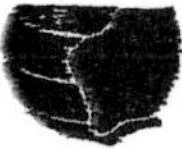

SSION SURVIVAL
WAY OF THE WOLF

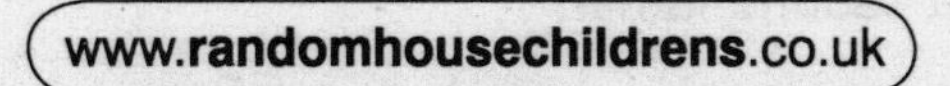
www.randomhousechildrens.co.uk

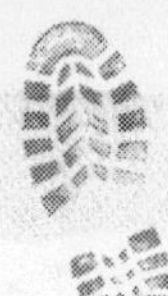

CHARACTER PROFILES

Beck Granger

At just thirteen years old, Beck Granger knows more about the art of survival than most military experts learn in a lifetime. When he was young he travelled with his parents to some of the most remote places in the world, from Antarctica to the African Bush, and he picked up many vital survival skills from the remote tribes he met along the way.

Uncle Al

Professor Sir Alan Granger is one of the world's most respected anthropologists. His stint as a judge on a reality television show made him a household name, but to Beck he will always be plain old Uncle Al – more comfortable in his lab with a microscope than hob-nobbing with the rich and famous. He believes that patience is a virtue and has a 'never-say-die' attitude to life. For the past few years he has been acting as guardian to Beck, who has come to think of him as a second father.

David & Melanie Granger

Beck's mum and dad were Special Operations Directors for the environmental direct action group, Green Force. Together with Beck, they spent time with remote tribes in some of the world's most extreme places. Several years ago their light plane mysteriously crashed in the jungle. Their bodies were never found and the cause of the accident remains unknown . . .

Tikaani

Tikaani belongs to the Anak, one of the Inuit peoples native to Alaska, although he has started to forget the ways of his people. As a boy his father sent him away to Anchorage so that he could learn the ways of the modern world. These days Tikaani is more interested in iPods and the delights of the modern world than he is in the oral tradition and culture of Anakat.

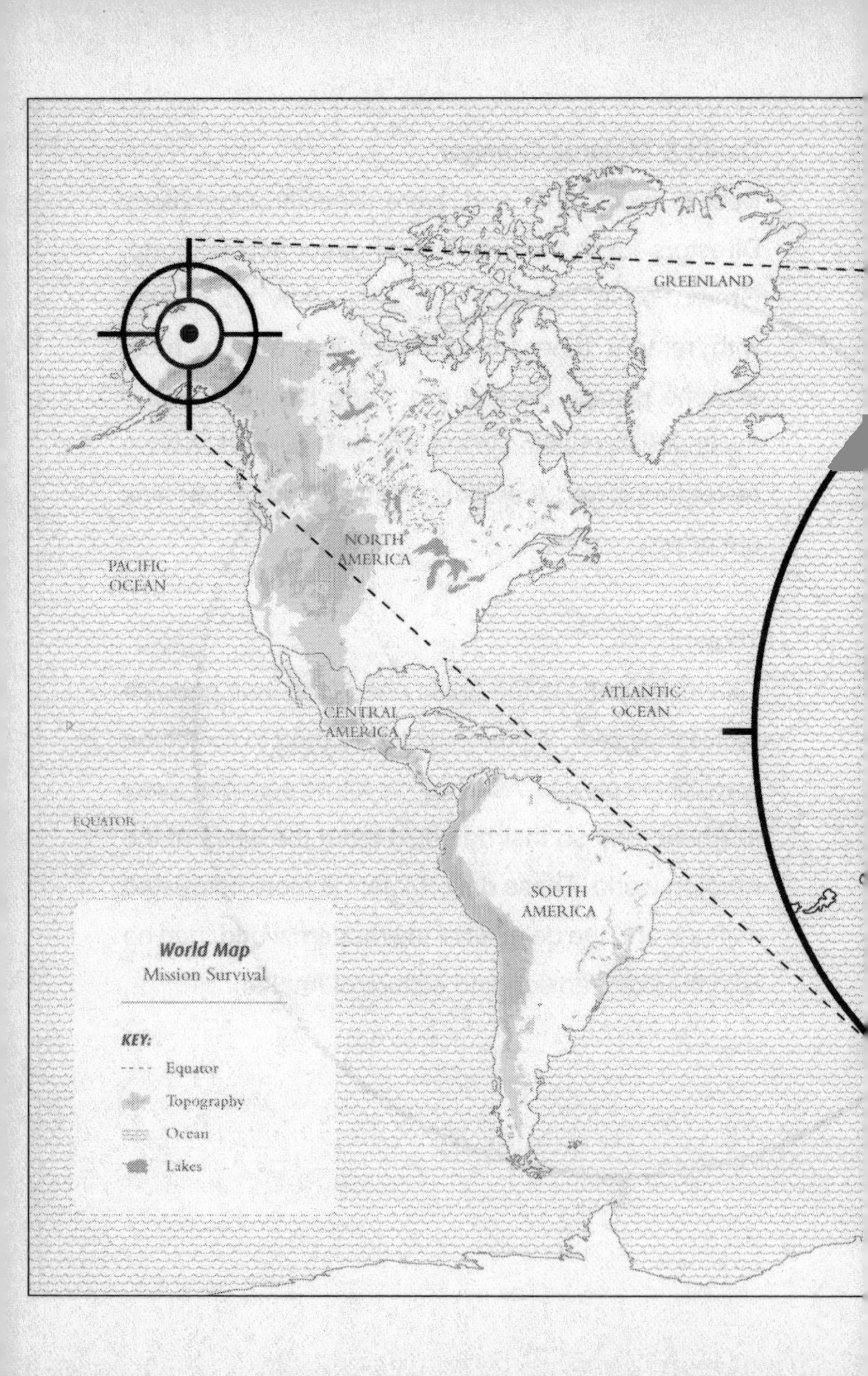
GREENLAND
PACIFIC
OCEAN
NORTH
AMERICA
ATLANTIC
OCEAN
CENTRAL
AMERICA
EQUATOR
SOUTH
AMERICA
World Map
Mission Survival
KEY:
Equator
Topography
Ocean
Lakes

ARCTIC OCEAN
BROOKS RANGE
SEWARD PENINSULA
ALASKA
ANCHORAGE
CANADA
GULF OF ALASKA
PACIFIC OCEAN
EQUATOR
OCEANIA
SOUTH PACIFIC OCEAN
ANTARCTICA

MISSION SURVIVAL

HAVE YOU READ THEM ALL?

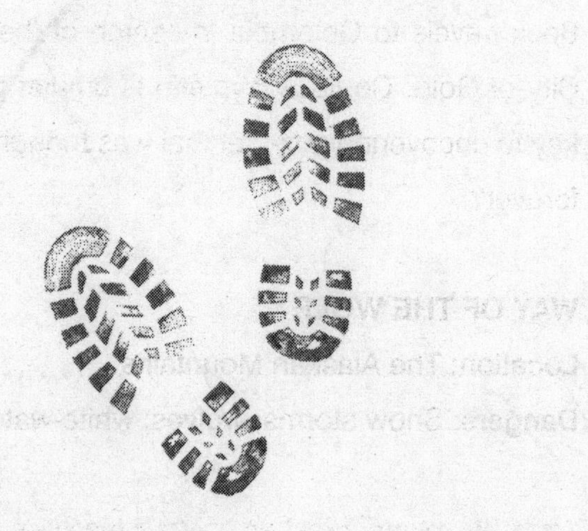

GOLD OF THE GODS

Location: The Colombian Jungle

Dangers: Snakes; starvation; howler monkeys

Beck travels to Colombia in search of the legendary City of Gold. Could a mysterious amulet provide the key to uncovering a secret that was thought to be lost forever?

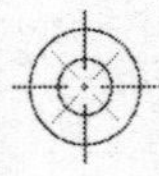

WAY OF THE WOLF

Location: The Alaskan Mountains

Dangers: Snow storms; wolves; white-water rapids

After his plane crashes in the Alaskan wilderness, Beck has to stave off hunger and the cold as he treks through the frozen mountains in search of help.

SANDS OF THE SCORPION

Location: The Sahara Desert

Dangers: Diamond smugglers; heatstroke; scorpions

Beck is forced into the Sahara Desert to escape a gang of diamond smugglers. Can he survive the heat and evade the smugglers as he makes his way back to safety?

TRACKS OF THE TIGER

Location: The Indonesian Wilderness

Dangers: Volcanoes; tigers; orang-utans

When a volcanic eruption strands him in the jungles of Indonesia, Beck must test his survival skills against red-hot lava, a gang of illegal loggers, and the tigers that are on his trail . . .

CLAWS OF THE CROCODILE

Location: The Australian Outback

Dangers: Flash floods; salt-water crocodiles; deadly radiation

Beck heads to the Outback in search of the truth about the plane crash that killed his parents. But somebody wants the secret to remain hidden – and they will kill to protect it.

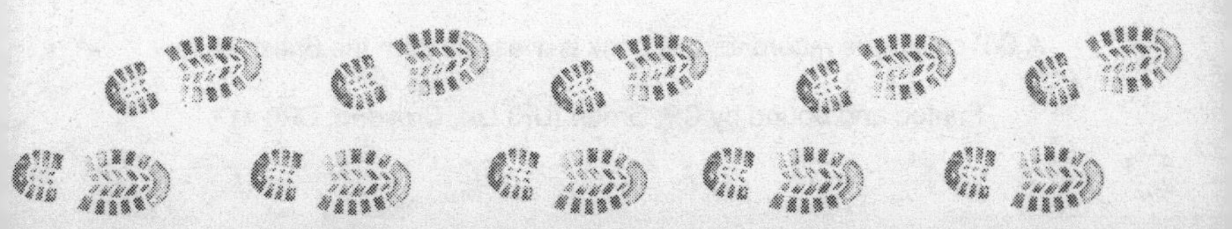

WAY OF THE WOLF
A RED FOX BOOK 978 1 862 30480 2

First published in Great Britain by Red Fox
an imprint of Random House Children's Publishers UK
A Random House Group Company

This edition published 2009

9 10 8

The Random House Group Limited supports The Forest Stewardship Council® (FSC®), the leading international forest-certification organisation. Our books carrying the FSC label are printed on FSC®-certified paper. FSC is the only forest-certification scheme supported by the leading environmental organisations, including Greenpeace. Our paper procurement policy can be found at www.randomhouse.co.uk/environment

Set in Swiss 721 BT

RANDOM HOUSE CHILDREN'S PUBLISHERS UK
61–63 Uxbridge Road, London W5 5SA

www.**randomhousechildrens**.co.uk
www.**randomhouse**.co.uk

Addresses for companies within The Random House Group Limited can be found at:
www.randomhouse.co.uk/offices.htm

THE RANDOM HOUSE GROUP Limited Reg. No. 954009

A CIP catalogue record for this book is available from the British Library.

Printed and bound by CPI Group (UK) Ltd, Croydon, CR0 4YY

MISSION SURVIVAL

WAY OF THE WOLF

BEAR GRYLLS

RED FOX

To my eldest son, Jesse.

Such a special boy.

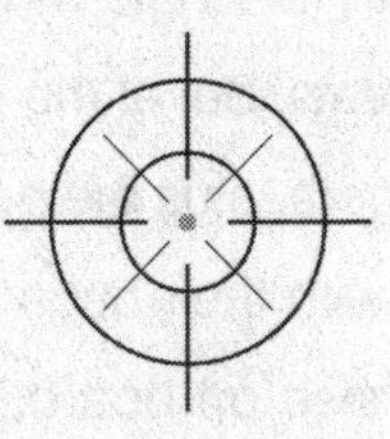

CHAPTER 1

The small plane crawled across the landscape like an insect over a tablecloth.

Beck Granger peered out at the patchwork of Alaskan wilderness thousands of feet below. It was spring and the thaw was all but complete. Not long ago it would have all been a smooth white, a land of ice and snow. Now he could see fir trees, grass, moss. Streams and rivers ran with crystal-clear meltwater. Endless shades of green, all tied together with fine silver threads.

Beck pressed his face to the window. He could just see the blur of the single propeller. The plane was a Cessna 180. Beck's Uncle Al, sitting in front next to the pilot, had told him it was the workhorse of the far north. It had a streamlined body like a plump fish suspended beneath its single wing. The cabin had a grand total of six seats, but at the moment there were only three passengers, plus the pilot. The back of the plane was stuffed with their bags and equipment.

Like everyone else on board, Beck was wearing large padded earphones. Without them the noise of the engine would have made talking to anyone impossible. Even with them on, the vibration rumbled like a tumbledryer in his guts.

A burst of static in his ears meant that the pilot had switched on the intercom.

'I'm adding an hour to the journey, guys.' She was a cheerful woman, middle-aged and stocky. You could see that she was descended from people who had made a home in this wilderness. 'There's bad weather ahead over the mountains and I intend to go right round it. It's way too much for this little plane.' The static went away again, and at the same time the plane began to tilt.

'OK,' Beck called, but he hadn't switched on his own intercom and his voice was lost in the roar of the engine.

The plane turned and brought the mountains into

view through the side windows. Beck looked out at them with respect. The thaw only reached part way up them. Maybe it never got higher. The trees grew part way up too, and then stopped abruptly in a ragged line, as if the mountains had shrugged them off as they burst from the ground. After that there was just grey rock clawing at the sky from beneath a thin white sheet of snow and ice.

The storm sat on top of the mountains like a wild creature feasting on the peaks, which were lost in a dark, whirling cloud. It was quite literally a force of nature: Beck could see why the pilot didn't want to risk her little plane against it. It was like coming across a bear in the wild. You didn't push your luck – you just took another route. That way everyone lived happily.

More static meant that the pilot was going to speak again.

'The good news is, the storm's not coming towards us. It's heading away but I don't want to catch it up. We're going to be a bit delayed doing this detour. I sure hope Anakat's worth it.'

'It will be,' Uncle Al promised. 'Trust me.'

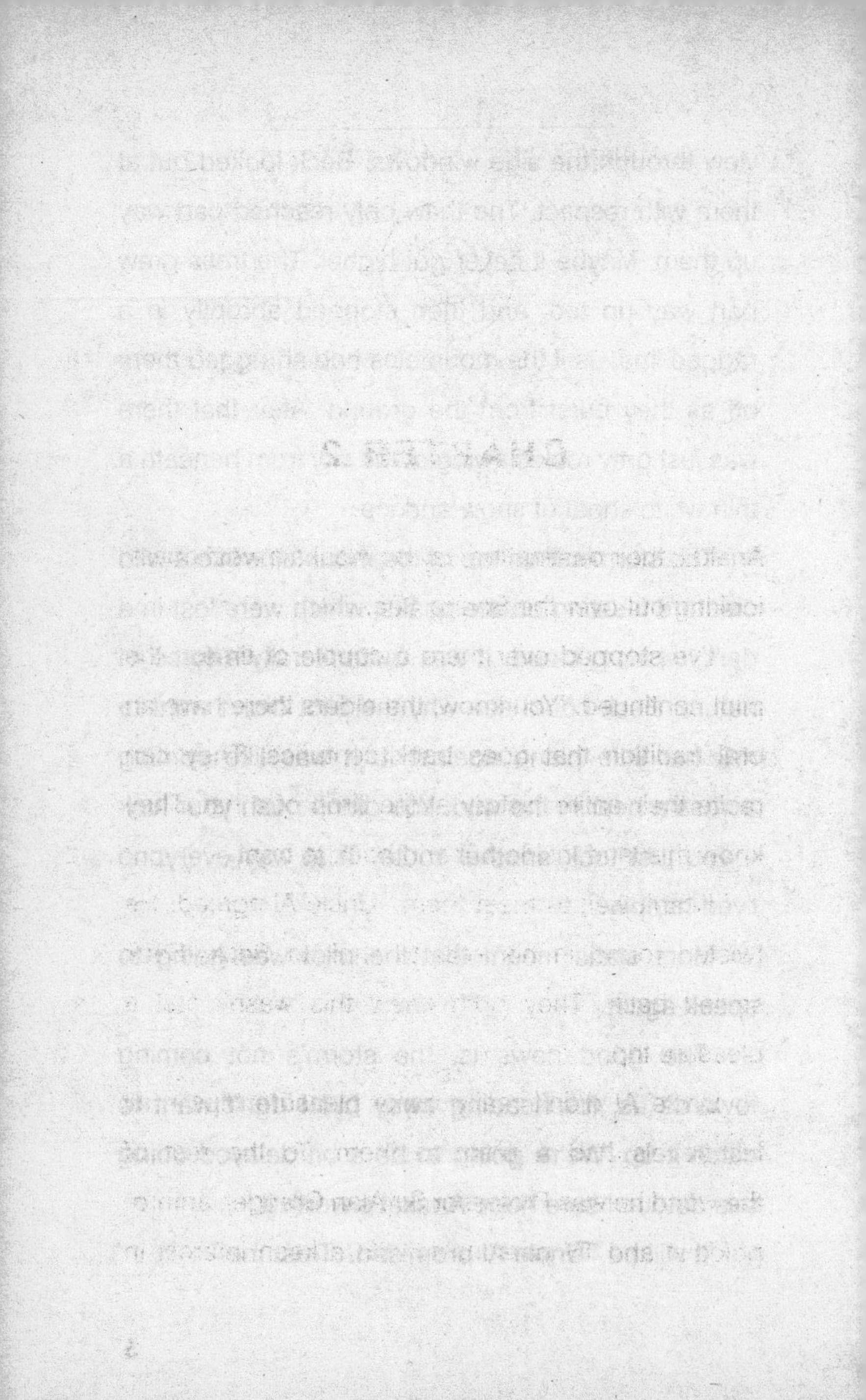

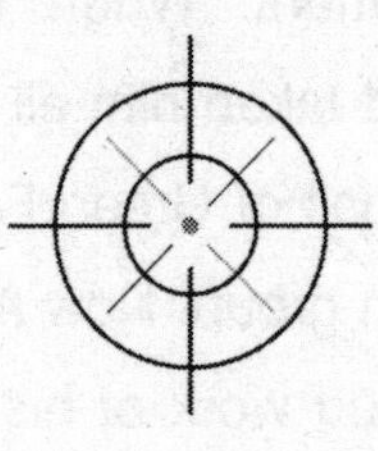

CHAPTER 2

Anakat, their destination, lay on Alaska's west coast, looking out over the Bering Sea.

'I've stopped over there a couple of times,' the pilot continued. 'You know, the elders there have an oral tradition that goes back centuries. They can recite their entire history at the drop of a hat. They know this land inside out and back to front.'

'I can't wait to meet them,' Uncle Al agreed. He twisted round in his seat to wink at Beck. Beck smiled back. They both knew this wasn't just a pleasure trip.

Uncle Al didn't really make pleasure trips – all his travels had a point to them. To the rest of the world he was Professor Sir Alan Granger, anthropologist and TV personality with a keen interest in environmental matters. When they were alive, Beck's parents had taken him all over the world in their travels on behalf of Green Force, the environmental direct action group. Now Al was determined to carry on the good work of his younger brother, Beck's dad.

'With all due respect to the National Curriculum,' he had once said to Beck, 'you'll learn a lot more this way.'

That, as Beck recalled, had been as they flew out to the Australian Outback to live with a community of Aboriginals . . .

He gazed back at the landscape outside. It looked very different to the baked desert of Western Australia but in some way it was very similar. This too was a world where Mother Nature ruled. Her word was law. An unprepared human being would be swallowed up and never seen again. It looked beautiful, but it was harsh and hostile.

But a *prepared* human being . . . ah, that was very different. A prepared human being could live in harmony with nature down there and never want for anything. The Inuit – the people who lived up here in the northern latitudes – spread from Alaska to Greenland; they had been managing it for thousands of years. That was why things like the oral tradition and culture of Anakat were so important. You could never learn it through books or off the web. You had to *live* it.

Beck and Uncle Al had flown from London to Seattle in a brand-new, wide-body airliner. Seattle-Tacoma International Airport was like a small space-age city, sparkling and modern. Then they had caught a plane to Anchorage, smaller and more crowded. And finally they had been picked up by the Cessna for the four-hour flight out here, across a landscape that hadn't changed in thousands of years. With each stage of the journey, Beck had felt he was shedding something he didn't need; one more layer of the twenty-first century.

Someone tugged at his elbow. Beck turned away from the window to look at the plane's third passenger. The twenty-first century's greatest fan.

Tikaani was in the seat next to Beck's. Like Beck he was thirteen years old. His accent was pure American, but one look at his features and his sleek dark hair told you where his ancestry lay. He belonged to the Anak, one of the Inuit peoples native to this area. In fact Tikaani's father was the headman of Anakat. He was a forward-thinking man and had decided the village's isolation couldn't last. Someone had to go out and learn the ways of the modern world.

So Tikaani had been bundled off to school in Anchorage. When Beck and Uncle Al stopped off there, Al's contacts in Anakat had called and asked if they could pick up the boy for the last leg of their journey.

Rather than use the intercom, Tikaani just leaned close to Beck, pulled back the earphone and shouted.

'What are you looking at?'

Beck replied the same way, putting his head close to Tikaani's. 'This landscape!' he called. 'It's amazing!'

'Uh-huh . . .' Tikaani craned his neck to look out of Beck's window, but there was only polite interest on his face. He was just trying to be friendly. There wasn't anything down there he hadn't seen almost every day of his life. 'Right. Uh' – he waved the thin plastic sliver of Beck's iPod, which he had borrowed back in Anchorage – 'how do you make it shuffle?'

Beck fought the temptation to roll his eyes. He took the iPod gently out of Tikaani's hand and showed him how to scroll through the options on screen.

'Thanks!'

Tikaani sat back in his seat again. The iPod's thin wires disappeared inside the padding of his earphones. Beck smiled to himself and shook his head. Tikaani's father's plan to help his son learn the ways of the modern world had been a little too successful. For all Tikaani's Anak heritage, Beck suspected he would gladly drop the oral tradition and culture of Anakat down a deep dark hole and leave them there.

And perhaps he would get the chance, because his world was about to change in a way that even Tikaani's father had never dreamed of.

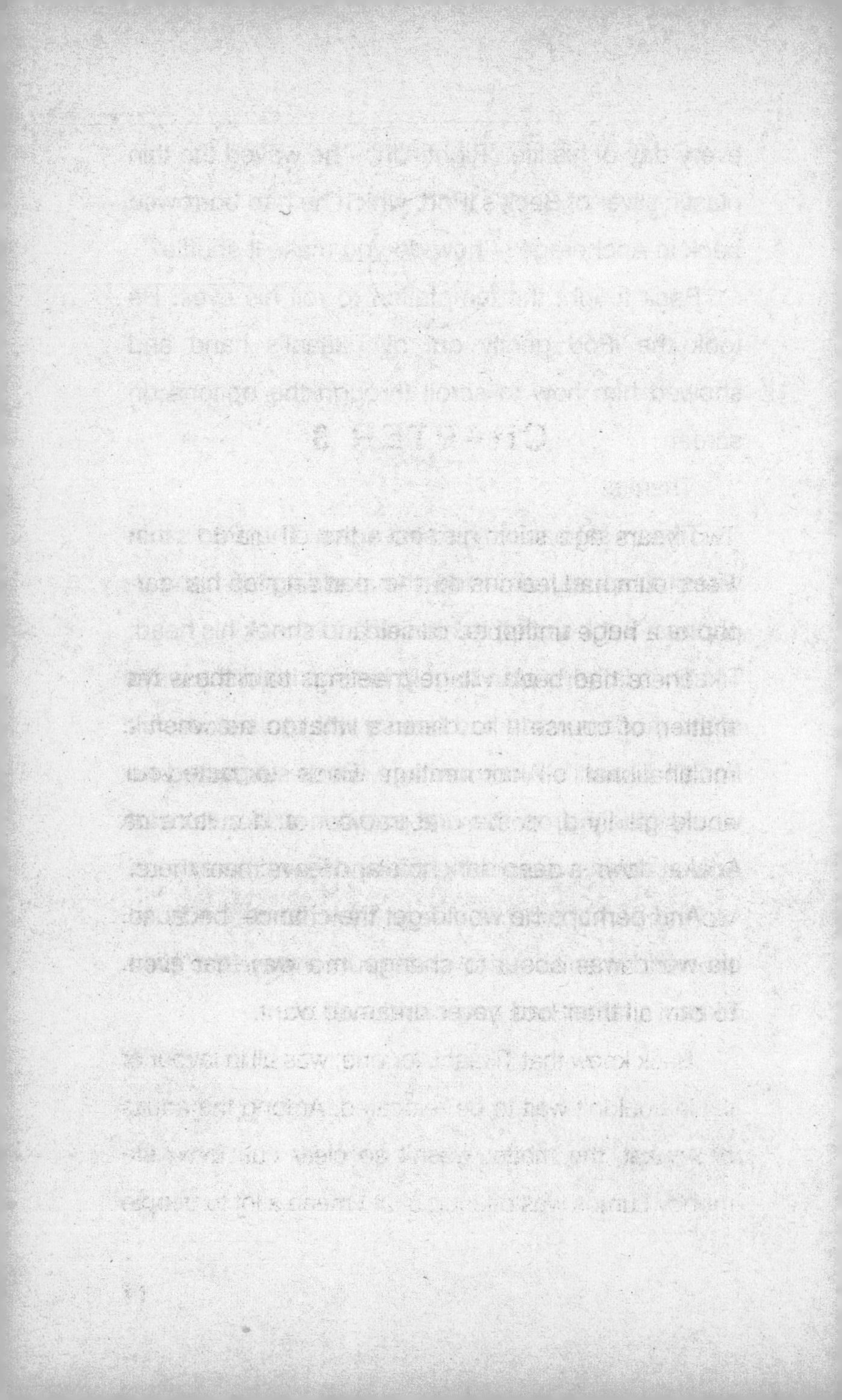

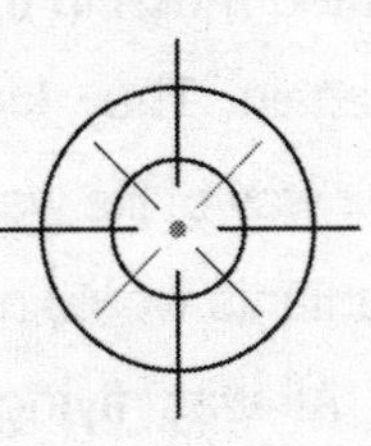

CHAPTER 3

Two years ago surveyors from the oil giant Lumos Petroleum had learned that Anakat sat slap-bang on top of a huge untapped oil field.

There had been village meetings to discuss the matter, of course – to discuss what to do when a multinational oil corporation wants to buy your ancestral land, destroy your way of life, relocate you . . . and sweetens the pill by offering every man, woman and child a brand-new home, with all modern amenities, and enough money in the bank to buy all the iPods you could ever want.

Beck knew that Tikaani, for one, was all in favour of it. He couldn't wait to be relocated. Among the adults of Anakat, the matter wasn't so clear cut. Even the money Lumos was offering didn't mean a lot to people who had never wanted much in the first place. It was that oral tradition again. They knew that what they could lose from their way of life was priceless in a way that Lumos's accountants would never understand.

And so Uncle Al was flying up to film a TV documentary about the village and the traditional Anak way of life. If it all changed, then at least there would be some record of it. Even better, the programme would make more people aware of just what was going on.

Suddenly there was a huge *BANG* and the plane lurched. Beck clutched at the armrests of his seat. The plane stabilized again; the engine was still running smoothly. Tikaani was sitting bolt upright, staring ahead, his face pale. Beck forced a smile. Wow! They must have hit an air pocket, and how! For a moment he had thought—

The engine stuttered and the plane shook. And then Beck realized that a trail of dark smoke was streaming past his window. It was coming from the engine. It grew thicker as he watched, from an innocuous wisp to an evil dark cloud in the freezing air outside.

And now the plane was very clearly banking to one side. It steadied again, but Beck could feel his insides lurching. The plane was dropping, and fast.

'Something's blown.' The pilot's calm tones in the earphones had gone, replaced with professional crispness. 'Oil feed's not getting through and engine temp's way up. I'm going to put the nose down and hope the air cools her enough to restart.'

Hope!? Beck wanted to scream. With the plane plummeting out of the sky, he could do with something a little more concrete than that . . .

The static went away and all that was left in Beck's ears was the roaring of his blood. The engine had stopped. No noise, no vibration. He pulled off the earphones. Air rushed past the plane's hull.

All he could see through the front windows was ground. Beck could hear the pilot's calm, urgent tones. 'Mayday, mayday, mayday. Anchorage, this is Golf Mike Oscar . . .'

'Beck . . .'

Beck barely heard. He was staring at the approaching trees. *This must have been what it was like—*

'*Beck!*' Uncle Al had turned in his seat again and his shout broke into Beck's reverie. 'And you too, Tikaani.'

Tikaani was also staring ahead like a mesmerized rabbit. Al had to click his fingers in front of the boy's face to get his attention.

'Both of you. You know the emergency position. Adopt it now.'

Beck and Tikaani glanced at each other, and then without a word they bent over double in their seats, arms wrapped around their knees, and waited. Beck had no idea what was going through Tikaani's head but his own thoughts continued to run away with him.

This must have been what it was like for Mum and Dad.

Three years earlier, they had been in a plane like this. It had crashed in the jungle. The plane had been found; they had not. They were presumed dead.

It had never occurred to Beck until now that a plane crash isn't instant. Something falling out of the sky takes time to reach the ground. And all you can do if you're on it is wait, and try not to picture the ground approaching . . .

The engine roared into life again and the pilot pulled back on the column. A mighty force pressed Beck back into his seat as the plane lifted. Tikaani shouted with triumph. Beck felt the plane levelling off, and lifted his head just in time to see trees rise up in front and smash into them.

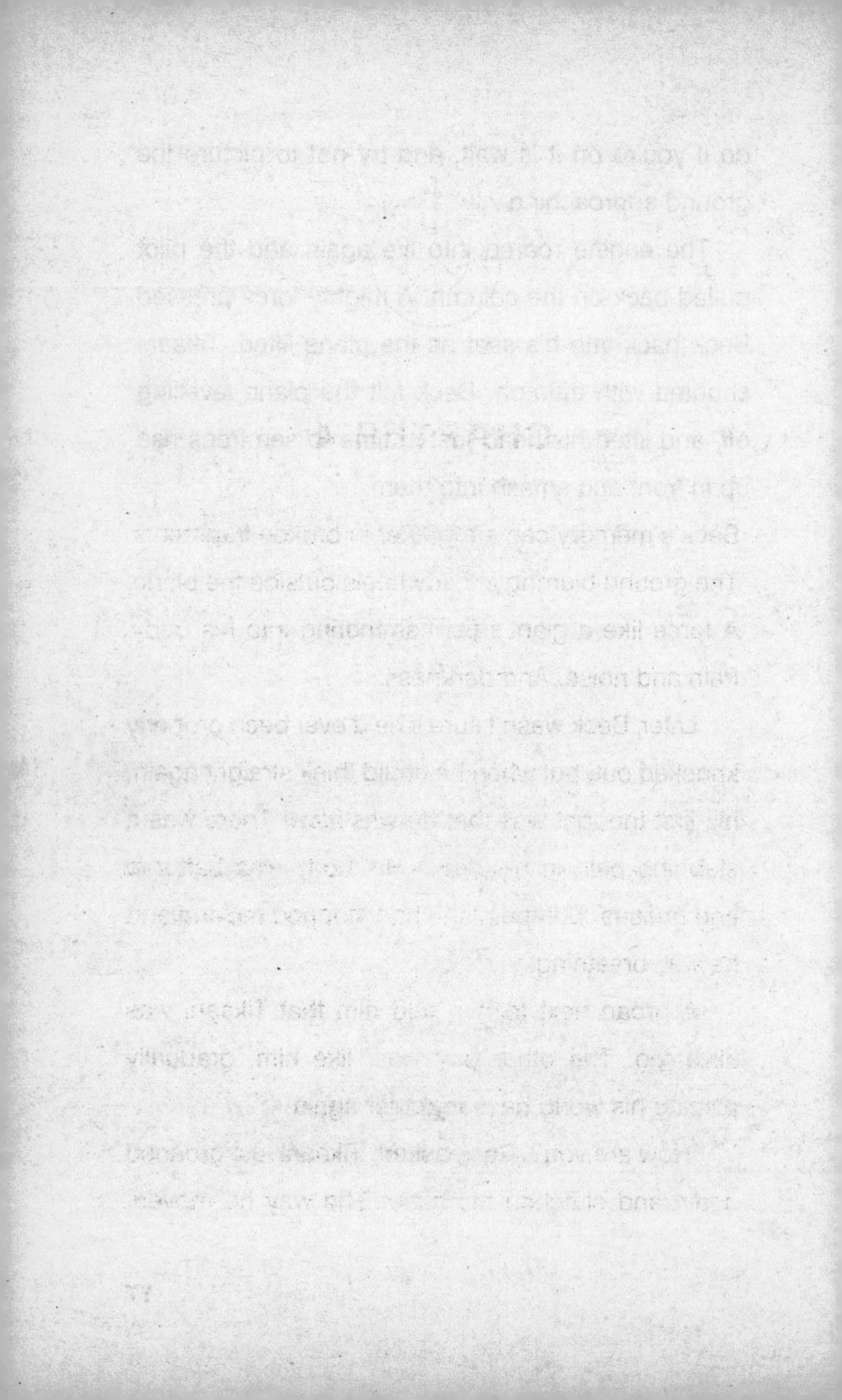

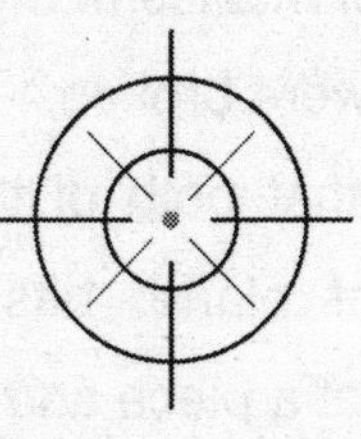

CHAPTER 4

Beck's memory came together in broken fragments. The ground blurring in cartwheels outside the plane. A force like a giant's fist hammering into his body. Pain and noise. And darkness.

Later, Beck wasn't sure if he'd ever been properly knocked out, but when he could think straight again, his first thought was that he was *alive*! There was a stabbing pain in his head. His body was battered and bruised. But the plane had stopped moving and he was breathing.

A groan next to him told him that Tikaani was alive too. The other boy was, like him, gradually piecing his world back together again.

'How are you?' Beck asked. Tikaani just groaned again and clutched his head. The way he moved, without any cries or intakes of breath, told Beck that at least no bones were broken.

Beck realized that both of them were covered in . . . bits. Bits of plane, bits of Perspex, bits of . . . He plucked at a piece and frowned. Wood?

Slowly, Beck looked up and forwards.

The plane had ploughed into a mass of undergrowth. Dead wood and branches, piled together by nature. The front of the plane had shattered and the pieces had been thrown back over the passengers inside.

'Uncle Al?' Beck asked. In the front seats, both Al and the pilot sat with their heads slumped. They weren't moving at all. Beck felt ice seize his heart as he realized that if the front of the plane had taken most of the impact, so had they. He scrambled out of his seat, ignoring the twinges that stabbed into him all over, and worked his way forward. He mentally ran through the four priority 'B's: Breathing, Bleeding, Breaks and Burns, then put his index and middle finger against Al's neck, just to one side of the Adam's apple. Then he breathed out in relief. There was a pulse, faint but regular.

Then Beck tried it with the pilot, pushing back her hair to get at her neck. There was nothing. He tried again, with a sinking feeling, but he could already feel her going cold. Reluctantly he craned his head a bit further forward to see. The crash had forced the control column right back. It had struck her in the chest, probably killing her instantly.

The entire instrument panel was wrecked. The radio dangled in a tangled mass of wires. They wouldn't be using that to call for help.

Now he was leaning forward he could also see that Al's legs were stained red. There was a nasty gash just above his uncle's knee and it was bleeding freely. That needed dealing with right away.

Tikaani was looking around with a glassy stare. He still wasn't quite taking it all in. Beck wondered with a stab of worry if he had concussion. Even if there were no broken bones, no internal damage, an untreated brain injury could kill him.

He remembered the first aid course from his cadet training.

'*There are four tests for concussion, gentlemen.*' The medical instructor had paced up and down in front of them, delivering his words like precisely targeted shots. '*Confusion! Memory! Concentration! Neurological! Repeat them please, Mr Granger.*'

'*Uh . . .*' Beck had said, taken by surprise.

The man had smiled without humour. '*A memory lapse! Or possibly confused, or maybe just not concentrating. Mr Granger is concussed, gentlemen. A bad start . . .*'

If Tikaani was OK, Beck could have really used his help. If he was concussed, all Beck could do was help him to rest. Beck had to know, now, which it was. He climbed back to face Tikaani and grabbed his head, making him turn so that he could look into his eyes. Both pupils were the same size, which was a good sign. That was the first Neurological test.

'What's your name?' Beck demanded. That came under Confusion.

'Uh . . . Tikaani . . .'

Beck moved on to Concentration: 'Give me the months of the year, backwards, starting from December.'

'Uh . . .' Tikaani's face creased with concentration.

'December . . . November . . . Sept— no, October—'

'OK, OK.' Beck let go of his head. 'Close your eyes and touch your nose.' That was also Neurological.

Tikaani did exactly as he was told without any difficulty. Then he opened his eyes and prodded Beck's nose as well.

'I can do that too,' he said. Beck grinned. It didn't come into any of the tests he could remember but it looked like Tikaani's thought processes were all present and intact.

'Yeah, you're OK,' Beck agreed with relief. 'We've got to get Uncle Al out of here. Let's see what's outside.'

He had to force his way past Al to get to the door. He tried it but it was jammed solid. He pushed harder but he could see that it was held fast by the undergrowth outside. The pilot's door was the same. He was never going to get it open. The only way out was through the smashed front window.

Beck slowly worked himself out of the front of the plane, until he was standing on top of the fuselage. Immediately he was out of the cabin's confined space, he felt the cold wind and shivered. They all had coats in the plane and would need to wear them. He looked around to take in where they were.

The plane was half buried by dead undergrowth. Looking around, he could see they were at one end of a clear patch of ground, in an area of tundra and pine forest. The plane had carved out a groove in the ground behind it and fragments were flung about. The undercarriage had snapped off as the plane hit. The wings were shattered stubs. The engine ticked as it cooled down.

There was a whistle down by Beck's feet. Tikaani had poked his head out of the shattered window and was gazing around at the destruction. Then he looked up at Beck and swung a small green box out onto the top of the plane.

'I found the first aid kit.'

'Great, thanks.' Beck ducked back down into the plane. 'Give me a hand with Uncle Al.'

Back in the cabin, the pilot was still strapped into her seat and Beck gave her a silent apology. It seemed indecent just to ignore her, so he covered her up with the plane's fire blanket. Then they turned their attention to Al.

The easiest part was releasing his straps. Then, as gently as they could, the two teenage boys had to manoeuvre a fully grown man out of the narrow hole left where the windshield had been.

The nose of the plane was much too small to lay Al out on and there was too much dead wood around to put him down on the ground. They had to take him out across the top of the plane. First they turned him round inside the cabin. Then, with Beck outside pulling and Tikaani inside pushing, they got him halfway through the broken windshield on his back. Finally they could fold him forwards at the waist over the top of the cabin. With more pushing and pulling, Al finally was out of the plane altogether and lying on top of the fuselage. Beck slid down to the ground near the rear of the plane while Tikaani held Al steady, then took his uncle in a fireman's lift over his shoulders. He was still knee-high in undergrowth so he kicked his way to clear ground and laid his uncle down.

At last he could inspect Al's wound properly.

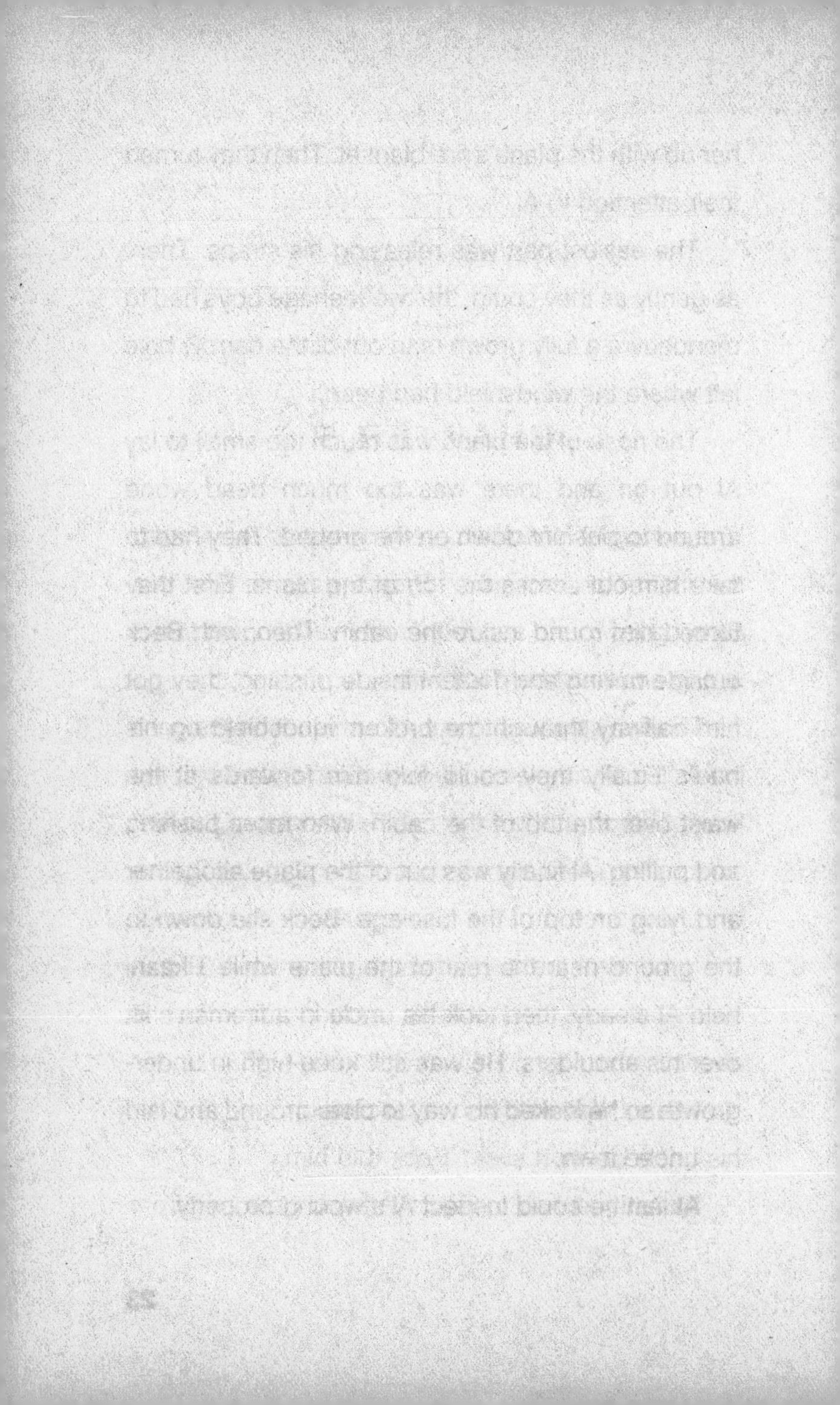

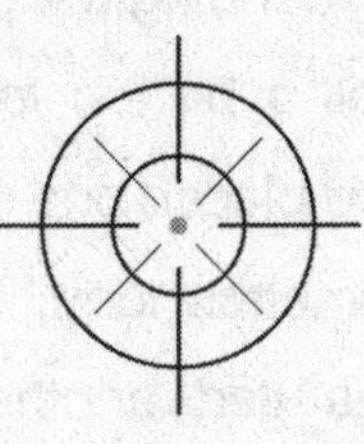

CHAPTER 5

'*The principles of first aid are very easy to remember,*' the instructor had said. '*Breath goes in and out. Blood goes round and round. Any variation on that is wrong and must be dealt with.*'

The first step was to put a tourniquet on the gash in Al's leg. A simple bandage wouldn't cope with the flow of blood at the moment. Beck opened the first aid kit and pulled out a length of bandage, which he wrapped once around Al's leg above the wound. Then he tied the two ends together in a simple overhand knot and looked around for what he needed next.

Tikaani was watching in fascination.

'I need a short stick,' Beck told him.

Tikaani just had to reach out and grab one from

the dead wood surrounding the plane. He handed it to Beck. It was still a bit too long so Beck broke it over one knee and placed one of the short lengths, about fifteen centimetres long, on the knot of the bandage. Then he tied another knot over that. Finally he twisted the stick to tighten the tourniquet.

'Wow. It's like turning off a faucet,' said Tikaani.

Beck took a moment to translate in his head. Americans said 'faucet'; Brits said 'tap'. 'That's the idea,' he said with satisfaction. And sure enough, the flow of blood did slow right down, as if a tap had been turned off. It would need relieving from time to time – some blood had to get through if Al was to keep the limb – but it dealt with the immediate blood loss. 'Could you hold the stick steady?'

And while Tikaani did that, Beck tied a final strip of bandage over it to hold it in place. Then he grinned up at the other boy. 'Not squeamish, are you?'

Tikaani was a little pale but Beck could understand that. He met Beck's gaze. 'Apparently not.'

'Good.'

Beck used the scissors in the first aid kit to cut

Al's clothes away from the wound. Finally he could see the gash properly. It was a good eight centimetres long, and deep. He wasn't sure what had made it – maybe something jagged from the shattered instrument panel. It started just above the knee and headed up from there. The blood was dark red and oozing. It was thickening, trying to coagulate and form a scab like a normal cut, but there was just too much of it.

Beck studied the cut as closely as he could without touching it. He was painfully aware that this was not a sterile environment and he didn't have any medical gloves. The last thing he wanted to do was introduce infection into the wound.

A tinkling sound of metal on glass caught his attention. The kit included a small bottle of disinfectant and a pair of tweezers. Tikaani was dipping the tweezers into the disinfectant.

'The wound must be clear of all debris, including dirt, dead skin and flakes of clotted blood,' Tikaani said, as if reciting something. 'Use tweezers sterilized with the disinfectant solution.'

'How did you know that?' Beck asked.

Tikaani grinned and nodded down at the box. 'There's instructions inside the lid. Here.' He passed the tweezers to Beck, who took them carefully, making sure he didn't touch the disinfected part.

'Thanks. We're going to need some water too.'

'I saw a bottle inside. Wait there a moment.'

Well, I'm not going anywhere . . . Beck thought as Tikaani clambered back inside the plane. He checked the wound again. It was fairly clear of debris but he still picked out a couple of blood clots and what looked like a bit of fabric from Al's trousers.

Tikaani was back with the bottle of water. 'Plus I got these,' he said. He dropped an emergency medical blanket and one of the seat cushions onto the ground. 'The lid says he should be kept warm against shock.'

'Never argue with the lid,' Beck agreed.

Tikaani slid the cushion under Al's head while Beck carefully poured more of the disinfectant straight into the wound. Tikaani hissed and winced with sympathy. Beck felt it too. He knew how much disinfectant could sting a simple cut; this would really be hurting Al, if Al was awake. The wound was as clean as it was going to get. He took the water from Tikaani and poured some over to rinse off the disinfectant.

'It'll just cause irritation if we leave it,' he explained as he handed the bottle back.

Finally he unwrapped a piece of gauze and got Tikaani to spread antibiotic cream on one side. Then Beck pressed the gauze onto the gash, cream side down, and tied it in place with more bandage wrapped around Al's leg. The sterile white fabric stained red immediately, but by and large the blood was now staying inside, just as the instructor had ordered.

'We can't just leave him on the ground,' Tikaani pointed out. He waved a hand around. 'This is tundra. There's permafrost a few inches down. He'll freeze.'

'Yup.' Permafrost meant that the soil was at zero degrees or below all year round. It wasn't something to lie on for any length of time. Beck looked about and his eyes settled on one of the plane's wings that lay nearby. 'But we can do something about that . . .'

The plane's wings were quite light. Between

them the boys could pick them up and lay them side by side. They made a platform to lay Al on – not very comfortable, but dry and solid; better than the icy ground.

Finally they worked Al into his coat and covered him with the blanket that Tikaani had found. Beck sat back on his haunches and looked at his uncle. He had done everything he could for the man. For the moment.

'So now what do we do?' Tikaani asked.

Beck sighed and stood up. 'Now we try and get out of this mess,' he said.

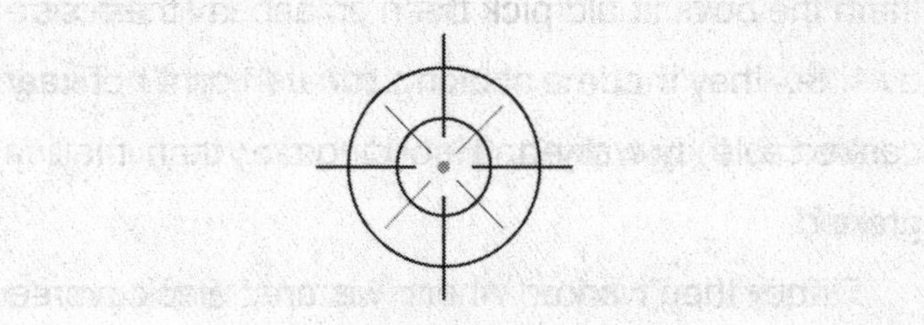

CHAPTER 6

They fetched their coats from the plane and set out to explore. It didn't take long.

North of here, Beck knew, the wind would be too harsh and the soil too icy for large plants like trees to grow. There would be nothing but tundra – a treeless plain of tough, scrubby grass and moss and lichen – all the way to the snow and ice of the North Pole. But here they were just far enough south for clusters of trees to gather together as if making a united, heroic effort to fight back the cold. They could stick their roots down through holes in the permafrost and survive.

The plane had come down right on the edge of one of those clusters. A few more metres and it would have crashed right into the firs and they would all have been smashed to pieces.

'So they'll come looking for us, right?' Tikaani asked as they walked. 'How long do you think it will take?'

'They don't know where we are,' Beck pointed out. 'We changed course.'

'But I heard the pilot do a mayday!'

'Yes,' Beck agreed, and repeated, 'But we changed course. I didn't hear her say that bit.' And he had no way of knowing if anyone had heard the mayday at all . . . Though he didn't say that to Tikaani.

'Well . . .' Tikaani looked thoughtful, but only for a moment. 'They've got satellites and' – he waved a hand vaguely – 'things. Haven't they?'

'Yeah, they have,' Beck agreed. And for all he knew Tikaani was right. Someone at Anchorage might have noticed the moment their plane vanished off the radar and the rescue services might be on their way as they spoke.

There again, they might not.

'We need to make ourselves easy to find,' he told Tikaani. 'Let's gather stuff together. Rocks. Bits of timber. Wreckage. Look, the plane's half buried – they may never see it from the air. We're going to mark out a huge great SOS, here on the ground . . .'

'Letters on the ground will just look tiny,' Tikaani pointed out.

Beck shrugged. 'So we make 'em *big*!'

And so they marked out an SOS with letters six or seven metres high. It took a good half-hour.

'They should see that, shouldn't they?' Tikaani asked with satisfaction.

'Uh-huh . . .' Beck cast an eye up at the sky. There was no sign of anyone looking for them yet . . . *But it's still early days*, he told himself. 'OK. Next we . . .'

And that was when the thought that had been lurking at the back of his mind ever since the crash – ever since *before* the crash – finally saw its chance and thrust itself forward. It chose its moment well. It smashed through his defences and brought him to a standstill.

Was it like this for Mum and Dad?

All Tikaani would have seen was Beck trailing off and gazing into the distance.

'Beck?' he asked anxiously. A pause, then again. 'Beck?'

But Beck barely heard him.

Had they survived the crash in the jungle? Had they done everything he was doing? But all for nothing, because they had vanished into the wild, never to be seen again—

'*Beck!*'

Tikaani's call brought him back with a shudder, and he vowed he wasn't going to do that again. There was no point trying to second-guess the past. It had happened and couldn't be changed. What mattered was the future, and what you did with it. Besides, in order to survive you needed to keep your spirits up. You needed good morale. You did *not* obsess over what *might* have happened.

'Next we find out exactly where we are,' he said decisively. 'There's a GPS in one of the bags. I make sure Uncle Al never travels without it.'

As they walked back to the plane, they could see something was different. Al had woken up. He had propped himself up on his elbows and was looking about.

'Hey, Uncle Al!' Beck and Tikaani ran forward.

Al's teeth showed white as he smiled up at them. 'Beck! And Tikaani too. Well done, both of you.' He spoke cautiously, occasionally stifling a grunt. Beck guessed he was in more pain than he wanted to admit. 'How's the pilot?'

The boys crouched down next to him and Beck explained the situation. Al didn't say much, though Beck knew he must understand how bad it was. There wasn't any need to say it out loud.

'There's a GPS—' Al started to say.

'I know. Hang on.' Beck climbed back down into the cabin and made his way to the rear of the plane. He rummaged through the bags until eventually he found what he was after.

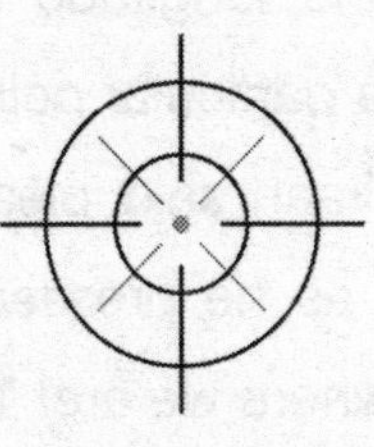

CHAPTER 7

Beck held a plastic box the size of a large phone. It could easily have been mistaken for a computer game. He switched it on and the flat screen glowed into life. The box held a silent conversation with satellites hundreds of miles overhead, fixing its position on the surface of the earth.

Beck tugged the pilot's map out of its compartment by her seat and went back to the others.

'Hey, cool,' Tikaani said when he saw the little box. He jostled Beck for a look at the screen.

Give him a bit of technology, Beck thought with a smile, *and the boy is happy!*

He handed Tikaani the map and the other boy spread it out on the ground. Beck read the co-ordinates off the GPS and Tikaani traced the lines of latitude and longitude on the map. They came together at a particular point.

'We're here,' Tikaani said, pleased. The other two leaned in to look as he pressed a finger into the paper. 'We know where we are! That's a good start, isn't it?'

'It always helps . . .' Beck agreed. Unfortunately he – and, he knew, Al – could see a whole lot that was wrong with the situation. Tikaani would be missing it.

On the map their position was just a few centimetres away from Anakat. Anakat was a square dot, the only square thing on the entire sheet of paper. The rest was curves and jagged lines. Anakat was manmade; the rest was natural. That square dot represented warmth and food and safety.

'And look,' Tikaani insisted. 'We're nearer to Anakat than to anywhere else. We could probably walk that in a day.'

'We could,' Beck agreed, 'if Uncle Al could walk anywhere.' But his finger traced the thick streak of contour lines on the map that lay between Anakat and where they were now. 'And if it was all flat. Unfortunately there are mountains in the way.'

They all glanced up and looked westward. The mountains were clearly visible, lying between them and Anakat like a mighty wall. The peaks shone brightly in the sun. They ran from north to south, and Anakat was almost due west. The direction was very easy to fix in the mind. The only fly in the ointment was a million tons of rock between them.

'If you include them,' Beck mused, 'and unfortunately we have to . . . two or three days' walk. Minimum.'

Tikaani only looked daunted for a moment. He gave the mountains another look, which told Beck he had grasped the scale of the problem. Even two or three days' walk wasn't the end of the world. But throw in the ice and snow and steep slopes of the mountains and it became a whole new ball game.

'OK . . .' Tikaani's voice trembled just a little and he said it again, more firmly. 'OK. But like I said before, they'll still come looking for us. They must be expecting us.'

'Um,' said Al. He suddenly sounded a little uncertain. 'Not necessarily.'

Now both boys were staring at him. It was his turn to shrug. 'Ours was an unscheduled flight. Lumos Petroleum's lawyers and publicists have been on our backs ever since the whole thing began. If they knew we were coming to Anakat, they'd be there first. I wanted to slip in under their radar, film the documentary before they knew anything. It's not a secret, of course . . . but I did sort of drop a few hints we'd be there next week, not this one.'

'Hey!' Tikaani exclaimed. 'This is the twenty-first century! Planes don't just disappear! OK, we were unscheduled but we must be on someone's log, somewhere. And my father knows we're coming.'

'Anchorage will have recorded our departure, and our flight plan,' Al agreed, 'but they have no reason to check whether we've arrived. Oh, they will notice. Eventually. But it could take days. And even your father doesn't know exactly when we were due. I didn't tell him when we took off in case Lumos got wind of it.'

Days . . . Beck thought. He glanced down at Al's leg, and up again at his uncle. The leg was only the obvious external wound. How smashed up was Al inside? His uncle was still pale and his voice was weak. There could be much worse damage that he couldn't see.

Beck wasn't certain that Al would be able to wait.

'Days . . .' Tikaani voiced Beck's thought. Forty miles off course and a three-day walk to safety. Rescue might take even longer than that to get to them. His shoulders slumped as the optimism drained away; he looked down. But then he lifted his head again and his face was set and grim.

'So what do we do?' he asked.

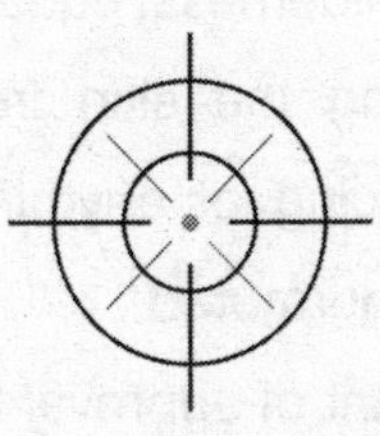

CHAPTER 8

The boys climbed into the plane once more and clambered over the seats to the back where the luggage was stored.

'So, what have we got . . . ?' Beck murmured.

One of the bags had their packed lunch in it – Beck knew that because he had been the one to pack it. It seemed like a long time since breakfast. He passed it back to Tikaani, then knelt down to have another look around. His eyes lit on a plastic toolbox, and he opened it up and rummaged inside. Among the wrenches and screwdrivers was a sheathed Bowie knife. He pulled it out and held it up so he could appreciate it.

The knife had a wooden handle, and a curved and pointed twenty-centimetre blade. It was a knife designed for the wilderness, equally good for cutting up meat, removing the skin from a carcass, or straightforward slicing of anything that needed it. 'Excellent,' Beck murmured.

He heard a grunt of approval from Tikaani.

'I had one of those,' the other boy said. 'I used it for show and tell at school and the teacher confiscated it. It frightened the city kids.'

Beck smiled to himself at the way Tikaani said *city kids*. However much Tikaani wanted to be a city kid himself, he couldn't quite shake off his heritage.

He tucked the knife in its sheath into his belt and looked around some more. Aha! A tarpaulin, folded and tucked away. He tugged it out and handed this back as well.

'Let's go,' he said. Behind him, Tikaani turned to climb out of the plane again. Beck tucked the toolbox under one arm and followed him.

Tikaani had asked: 'What do we do?' Beck broke the answer down into short term and long term. Short term: make a shelter, make a fire, find food and water. Make themselves as secure and comfortable as they could. Long term . . . well, he would see how the short term worked out. In the long term, rescuers might show up.

They could have used the plane for shelter, but the pilot was still in there and they couldn't have lit a fire without the risk of igniting the fuel. Besides, Al wouldn't be able to get in and out without help.

A boulder jutted out of the tundra a short distance from the plane, carried there by ice thousands of years ago and dropped when the ice retreated. With a bit of grunting and heaving, Tikaani and Beck moved Al carefully off the plane's wings; they carried them over and propped them up against the rock, overlapping so that no breeze could get through the space between them. That was the shelter.

With Beck's right hand linked with Tikaani's left, and arms around each other's shoulders, they formed a makeshift cradle and carried Al over to install him in his new home.

'Very nice.' Al lay back on the ground beneath the wings. They had covered it with fir branches and a layer of clothes to keep him off the tundra. 'Very nice indeed. The best house a man could ask for.'

'It's a traditional Inuit home,' Tikaani murmured ironically, looking at the wings. 'Aluminium is what we always use if we can't get caribou skin.'

Making the fire wasn't hard. They were surrounded by dry dead wood. Tikaani gathered up a pile of small, breakable bits of wood for kindling while Beck went looking for water and some other essentials.

Luckily, he didn't have to go far before he came across a tiny stream racing merrily through the wilderness. The water was cold and clear and Beck filled the two water bottles that he and his uncle always travelled with.

'What's that?' Tikaani asked a little while later as he dropped his kindling onto the ground. At the entrance to the shelter, Beck was making a heap out of what looked like wispy, grey-yellow hair.

'Old Man's Beard,' Beck explained. He cheekily held up a piece next to Al's face. 'See?'

Al swatted his hand away. 'Less of that!' he exclaimed.

'It's moss,' Beck explained. 'Not the wild clematis that we know as Old Man's Beard in England. Grows on trees, grows on rocks, burns very easily.'

Beck put a layer of Tikaani's kindling on top of the small pile, followed by a few larger pieces of wood. Tikaani looked on as he pulled out a bootlace hanging round his neck. Two bits of metal – a small rod and a flat square – dangled on the end.

Beck saw him watching. 'It's a fire steel,' he explained. 'I take this everywhere. You strike the rod with the scraper . . .' He demonstrated, and Tikaani flinched away from a shower of sparks. 'And, sparky, sparky. One thing I can do anywhere is set a fire.'

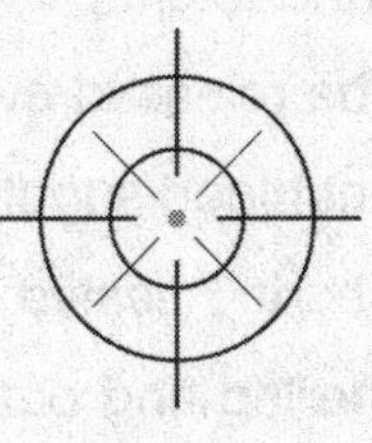

CHAPTER 9

Beck struck the fire steel again next to the small pile of kindling. Sparks settled on a couple of strands of Old Man's Beard and they started to burn, more a red glow than a flame. They twisted and writhed as the glow consumed them. A few seconds more and the dead moss was all but gone, but a thin flicker of flame licked against the kindling. A piece of wood snapped, another crackled as the fire took hold and gradually spread out. Now Tikaani grinned and crouched down with his hands held out to the heat.

'How's the leg?' Beck asked his uncle.

Al shifted himself towards the fire and looked thoughtfully down at the bandage. 'You did a good job, Beck. Thanks. Get more of the gauze ready. I'm going to release the tourniquet . . .'

Beck nodded and fetched the first aid box. The tourniquet had to be released eventually because a limb with insufficient blood supply will just go rotten. But if the wound hadn't sealed itself, blood would simply rush into the leg and out of the gash and it would need rebandaging.

'Could you . . . ?' Al asked. Beck held the stick steady while his uncle released the knot holding it in place. He loosened the tourniquet by half a turn and grunted, teeth clenched. All three of them looked carefully at the bandage. After a minute it obviously wasn't getting any redder.

Beck breathed out; Al refastened the tourniquet in its new, looser position.

'Give it another twenty-four hours and I'll take it off,' he said. He smiled with an effort at the boys. His face was white and drawn with pain but he seemed determined to be cheerful. 'Now, lunch?'

Lunch was a frugal meal of cold meat and biscuits. It did the job, but . . .

'This isn't going to last us for a few days,' Tikaani said unhappily.

'Hey, we're surrounded by food!' Beck told him.

Tikaani looked around. 'Yeah. Yummy grass followed by fir-tree dessert.'

Beck reached for the toolbox that lay nearby. He tipped out the contents and stood up with the empty container. 'Come on, I'll show you.'

Five minutes later they were in the woods. The boys crouched by a fallen log that was slowly disintegrating with age. Beck poked aside the layers of rotten bark with the knife tip and they fell away to show a cluster of brown, lens-shaped mushrooms, smooth and silky beneath the dirt.

'This is deer mushroom,' Beck told the other boy. 'It grows on dead wood and it's perfectly safe to eat.'

'Paluqutat,' Tikaani said unexpectedly. Beck looked up at him in surprise, and he shrugged. 'Hey, I used to help my grandma gather it up. It's just never been a main meal before.'

'OK . . .' Beck pried the rest of the deer mushrooms off the log and dropped them into the box. 'Well, we need plenty of this and also . . . Aha!'

He pushed aside the leaves of a nearby bush

and Tikaani saw a cluster of berries. They were black and half the size of plums.

'These are bearberries,' said Beck. 'They're very easy on the stomach and they fill you up, so . . .'

'What are you?' Tikaani asked as they set to stripping the bush of its load. 'Some kind of expert?'

'Expert?' Beck paused a moment. He didn't want to brag. 'I know a thing or two. I spent a month with a Sami tribe in Finland once – Mum and Dad were doing research there. It's not too different to this place.'

'So you've done this before? I mean, actually had to survive in the wilderness?'

'The wilderness? No.' Beck straightened up from the bush and looked around for more. 'The jungle . . . well, yes.'

'Hey? When?'

'Look around for more mushrooms,' Beck instructed. 'I'll see if I can find some more berries. When? Um . . . a couple of months ago . . .'

And so, while they gathered food together, Beck found himself telling Tikaani about his recent time in Colombia with his friends Christina and Marco.

Uncle Al had been kidnapped, and they'd had to get through miles of inhospitable, humid jungle to rescue him. As well as finding food they'd had to negotiate waterfalls and bullet ants and jaguars and a poisonous snake . . .

'You cut its head off? Just like that?' Tikaani was incredulous as Beck described his encounter with the deadly bushmaster.

Beck grinned. 'And ate it later.'

Tikaani whistled, impressed.

They found a cranberry bush bearing small, tart fruit. The berries exploded on the tongue in a burst of sourness, but they were still edible.

The boys went back to the plane with a box full of one variety of mushroom and two kinds of berries. Tikaani was looking a little more cheerful.

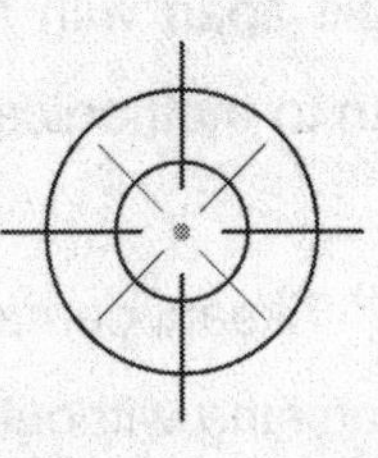

CHAPTER 10

By now it was early afternoon. They had been on the ground for several hours. There was still no sound of rescue – no faint, distant drone of an aeroplane or helicopter on a search pattern.

Beck's thoughts turned reluctantly to long-term plans. 'We need to unpack the plane,' he said.

And so Tikaani stood on the fuselage while Beck passed him the bags up from inside, and then chucked them onto the ground.

'Hey, I should get a job as a baggage handler!'

When everything was unloaded, Beck opened up the first bag. As he had expected, it was mostly clothes. Good. They had all packed several changes of gear – and that meant there was plenty to spare.

He picked up a shirt and thrust the knife into the

cotton fabric. It split apart with a satisfying tearing sound. Beck began to methodically reduce the shirt to shreds.

'Say what . . . ?' Tikaani demanded.

Al had been watching without comment, leaning back on his elbows. He hadn't needed Beck to explain his actions. 'Beck is taking precautions,' he explained, 'just in case the rescuers don't get here in time.'

'They won't,' said Beck. 'And you know it.' He carried on cutting.

'Beck,' Al said, and Beck heard something very like pleading in his voice. 'You know the procedure. If there's a crash, you stay with the wreck. You don't go wandering off. They're much more likely to see the plane than to see you, so you stay with it.'

'Yes, and usually you'd be right, but' – Beck nodded back at the plane – 'our plane's going to be practically invisible from the air. It's half covered already.'

Tikaani was looking from one to the other, utterly baffled. 'Did I miss half the conversation? Cutting up a few shirts will help us how?' he asked.

Beck smiled. 'I'm going to make rope. You always need rope in the wilderness.'

'Rope?'

'Sure. You plait and twist this all together, and you get some good, strong—'

'But . . . rope? Why do we need that?'

'Haven't you guessed?' Al asked him. 'Beck doesn't think they're going to come for us – and that means he'll have to go and get help. And unfortunately I'm not sure I can stop him.'

'We'll give it a few more hours,' Beck said, just in case Tikaani thought he was going to disappear into the wilderness there and then. 'See what happens in the morning.'

Tikaani looked at Beck with eyes that were comically round. And again, he darted his eyes over to the mountains – the biggest obstacle to any plan that involved walking.

'You really don't think they're coming?'

'Forty miles off course,' Beck reminded him. 'And practically no one has any idea we've even taken off yet. No, I think the only way they'll come looking for us is . . . if one of us goes and tells them to.'

* * *

By slashing up shirts and the plane's seat covers, Beck was able to make two good lengths of rope. They held together even when he and Tikaani pulled the two ends in opposite directions with all their strength. Then he checked the contents of the bags again for the clothes they were going to need.

'Hey, no problem there,' Tikaani said proudly. He indicated the coat he had been wearing since they got out of the plane. It was a thick, padded parka with a fur-lined hood. 'My aunt gave me this and I can stay warm in a blizzard in it.'

Beck took one look. 'Sorry, but . . . no.'

Tikaani's face fell. 'No? But it's warm!'

'It's too warm,' Beck told him. 'We're going to have to cross the mountains. That thing will weigh you down, and it'll be freezing, and you'll sweat, and the sweat won't be able to evaporate through that, and it will freeze and chill you. Water conducts heat away from the body much more quickly than air. No, you need lots of thin layers, so that you can add them or take them off as necessary, and the air can get at you and dry the sweat before you know it's there. Don't worry, I'll show you how.'

Tikaani looked ruefully at his parka, holding his arms out, then let them drop to his side. 'Sorry, Auntie . . .' he murmured.

'We're going to need walking sticks,' Beck said. 'Could you look around for a couple? They need to be straight, and strong, and not too heavy.'

'Walking sticks? You know, I have legs!' Tikaani pointed out.

'Sure, and they carry all your weight. A stick just takes a little of the weight off but it helps you add miles to your journey.'

Tikaani pursed his lips thoughtfully. 'My grandfather always used a stick. I thought he was just geriatric . . .'

Meanwhile Beck had thought of something else he could be doing. While Tikaani wandered off into the trees, he climbed back into the plane for the last time. He squeezed himself into the foot space by the rudder pedals, next to the pilot's shrouded form, and started to attack the wiring behind the control panel with the knife.

'Well, it's definitely not going anywhere now,' Tikaani said dolefully. He had returned with two likely candidates for walking sticks, and found Beck with a bundle of the plane's wiring in his hands.

'It's stronger than rope,' Beck said logically. 'You never know. What did you get? Hey, good choice!' he added when Tikaani held the sticks up for inspection.

Tikaani had chosen two branches, long and thin, but not so thin that they would bend under pressure. They only needed a bit of work with the Bowie knife – cutting off leaves, shaving down knots in the wood – to be suitable. Beck saw his words take root inside the other boy and lift his spirits a bit.

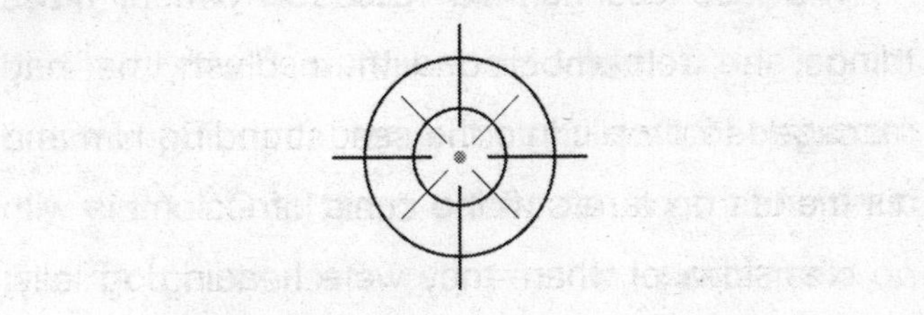

CHAPTER 11

'So, what's your plan, Beck?'

Al asked the question while Beck and Tikaani fixed up a basic meal from the plane's meagre stores. It was dinner time, though this far north there was still plenty of light. The meal finished off all the food they had brought with them. From now on all three of them would be living off the wilderness.

Beck unfolded the map again and took out the GPS. He frowned at the little bar on the screen that showed the battery status. It was low, and the nearest recharge socket would be in Anakat, where they were heading. He would have to use the device sparingly and, crucially, keep the batteries as warm as possible to help the power last.

The last time he had relied on one of these things, he remembered with a blush, he had managed to drop it into the sea, stranding him and his friends on a raft off the coast of Colombia with no clear idea of where they were heading. At least he wouldn't be doing that this time.

He found their position on the map again. This time he found a pen and a piece of paper and wrote down the GPS coordinates – but he also made an effort to memorize them – you never knew what might happen. If the little gadget's power didn't last, he was going to have to have them ready to pass on when they reached Anakat. He turned off the GPS and took out the batteries, wondering where he could put them for warmth – next to his skin would be best, but they had to be secure . . . There was nothing else for it: he stuffed them down his underpants and then turned to the map which the other two were studying.

'I noticed this earlier,' he said, tapping the map in three different places. 'Us. Anakat. Mountains. But see . . .'

Beck leaned very close and the others craned

their heads nearer. There was a small gap in the mountains – a tiny white thread on the paper.

'There's a very narrow pass. If we can get through that, it'll save us climbing hundreds of extra metres. And now it's spring – well, it should be clear of snow. We can do this.'

'"We",' Al repeated thoughtfully. 'I still don't like that word. In fact I don't much like the word "you" either. Beck, we should all stay together. It will be hard but they will come for us eventually, and you know enough to keep us all alive—'

'No,' Beck said bluntly, 'I know enough to keep Tikaani and me alive. I'm not a doctor and that's what you need. You're too pale and I can hear your breathing rattle. It's not just a cut in your leg – you're worse than you're letting on. You need help. Look at me, Uncle Al. Look me in the eye and tell me I'm wrong.'

Al looked him in the eye, but that was all. He had never told Beck a lie in his life and he couldn't start now. They both knew Beck was right.

Beck remembered what he had thought, in the plane, about a prepared human surviving in the wilderness. He hadn't been wrong. But the wilderness was unforgiving to the sick and the old. Animals that were sick or old didn't die quietly in bed, or plugged into life support, surrounded by grieving relatives. They died quickly because they were weak and something killed them.

'And,' he added reluctantly, 'Tikaani comes with me.'

He had thought about this a lot. He looked Al in the eye again and, after a pause, his uncle nodded slightly. Beck knew Al had come to the same conclusion. If just Beck went for help, and Al and Tikaani stayed, and Al died . . . Tikaani probably wouldn't last five minutes on his own.

'Hey, yeah!' Tikaani said. He looked from one to the other. Beck could see the uncertainty on his face; he knew how brave his friend was being. Tikaani understood what the Alaskan tundra was like. Freezing winds. Snow and ice up in the mountains. Quite possibly bears and other hazards.

'I mean,' Tikaani added, as if to reassure himself, 'I can help. Can't I?'

'Sure you can,' Beck agreed, with a smile. Tikaani's smile back was brave and flattered.

'When will you leave?' Al asked.

'First light.'

'Then give it an hour. If they're looking for us, they'll start at first light too. Wait an extra hour. If there's still no sign . . .'

He didn't need to finish the sentence.

'An hour after first light,' Beck agreed. 'Then we go.'

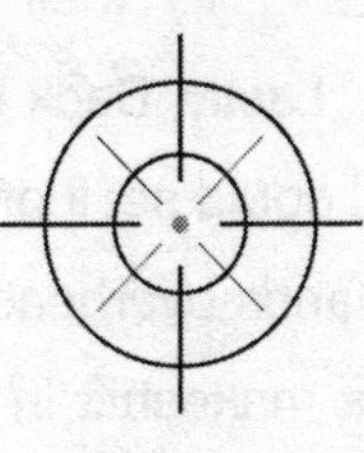

CHAPTER 12

In fact they gave it an hour and a half. First light this far north was very early indeed. By five o'clock it was as bright as mid-morning back home. And, try as they might, they still couldn't see or hear a thing that wasn't natural. In other words, no rescuers.

Beck and Tikaani spent the extra time gathering wood for Al. The older man could move about a little, but the more time he spent resting the more chance he had of recovering. The fire burned brightly just outside his little shelter and the spare timber was piled within easy reach. At the back of the lean-to Beck had left the two water bottles he had filled at the stream – now carefully topped up – spare clothes, and all the food they had gathered so far. The boys would gather more food for themselves as they walked, and fill their plastic bottles at streams and rivers. Lastly, Beck left a red flare from the plane so that Al could set it off to alert rescuers if he heard search planes overhead.

The shelter was makeshift in the extreme, but it would keep Al out of the wind, and as warm and dry as possible. It should certainly keep him alive for the three days that Beck estimated it would take them to reach Anakat – if, that is, whatever was damaged inside Al didn't decide to rupture so that he bled to death. Beck consciously didn't think about that because there was nothing he could do about it.

'OK,' said Al at last. 'Let's have a final look.' He ran his eyes up and down the two boys.

Two of the bags in the plane were rucksacks, so they had emptied them out and filled them with their supplies: the ropes, the tarpaulin, the plastic bottles Tikaani had found on the plane, a few items from the medical kit – cotton wool, antiseptic cream, a bandage – and a complete change of dry clothes each.

By plundering all the clothes in all the bags – their own, Al's and the pilot's – Beck had been able to get them both kitted out in trousers, T-shirts, sweatshirts and fleeces. Plenty of layers, as he had told Tikaani, combining together to keep them warm. They had light waterproof coats on top; good sturdy boots on their feet; and hats and mittens.

'You'll do your ancestors proud, Tikaani,' Al added.

Tikaani pulled a wry smile. 'My ancestors would want to know why I wasn't wearing skins cured the traditional way, in urine. I think I'd rather do it this way.'

Al chuckled, but he sounded weak and Beck prayed for the thousandth time that his strength would last. Beck gave him a final hug and Tikaani shook hands awkwardly.

'You'll do,' said Al with a brave smile. 'Now go and get me rescued.'

An hour later, Beck found proof that they weren't the only living creatures walking in the woods.

The way had been easy going so far. The trees weren't thickly clustered on the tundra, and if there were any bushes, then the boys could simply walk around them. Their boots scuffed through a soft carpet of dead pine needles. Beck couldn't decide if it was like a huge meadow with trees growing in it, or a huge fir forest with large, grassy clearings.

One tree in particular caught his attention at one point. It was a fir tree and its bark hung down in shreds. Huge gouges had been cut into the trunk by something almost three metres tall – considerably bigger than either of the boys.

'Uh-oh,' he muttered. 'I wondered when we'd find one of these.'

'That's bear sign,' Tikaani said flatly, studying the damaged wood.

Bear sign indeed, Beck agreed inwardly. The bear had treated the tree like a giant scratching post. Claws fifteen centimetres long had shredded the wood like it was cardboard. The animal had been looking for insects under the bark.

He glanced at his friend. 'Have you seen bears before?'

He wasn't surprised Tikaani recognized it for what it was. Beck had been trained in what to do in bear country but had never actually met one.

Tikaani, growing up in Anakat, could hardly not have.

'Sometimes, yeah, a long way away. But then I always do *this*.' Tikaani whacked his stick against the nearest trunk and grinned.

Beck nodded. Tikaani had described the best way to travel in bear country. Make plenty of noise and the bears would probably – *probably* – keep away.

'They stay away from crowds and they don't come into town at all,' Tikaani went on. 'Which is just one reason why I really prefer living somewhere like Anchorage. Apart from, you know, the hot and cold running water and the central heating and the electricity that doesn't go off because the generator broke down *again*.'

Beck spotted one obvious flaw in Tikaani's logic . . .

'We're not a crowd and we're not in a town,' he pointed out. 'They might not be so scared of us.'

Tikaani pulled a face. 'OK, plan B: you keep eye contact, you back away slowly. Dad says that sometimes a bear will stand on its back legs but that just means it's curious and wants to get a better look at you. It doesn't mean it's going to attack. And sometimes, too, they'll bluff a bit. They'll chomp their teeth and they'll slap the ground like they're going to attack, but they're just trying to frighten you. Which,' he added with feeling, 'would work. I'd be terrified.'

Beck nodded again. So far, so good. 'They just want to work out who's dominant,' he explained. 'But what if, after all that, they still come at you? Like, it's a mother bear and you just got between her and her cubs?'

Which is about the stupidest place to be in the whole world . . . Mother bears, Beck knew, weren't interested in dominance. Just in seeing off the threat.

Tikaani's pleased expression froze. Then he thumped the nearest tree twice as hard with his stick. 'OK. Then we, uh . . . we . . .' He looked pleadingly at Beck, who raised an eyebrow. 'Run away?'

Oops. It looked like they had got to the edges of Tikaani's education.

'Only if you want to be dinner,' Beck said. 'They can out-run you, out-swim you . . .'

Tikaani glanced up at the nearest tree.

'. . . and definitely out-climb you,' Beck finished.

'So what do we do?' Tikaani muttered.

'OK. Brown bears . . .'

'Grizzlies.'

'Grizzlies, call 'em whatever – for them, you lie down.'

'Huh?' Tikaani stared at him.

'Play dead. Curl up, lie on your side' – Beck clasped both hands behind his neck – 'and put your hands like this. You're protecting all your squishy bits—'

'Is that a technical term?'

'– and you're really showing it you're not a threat. But you have to stay like that. They may try to chew your pack or knock you about a bit. If you put up any kind of fight, that's just going to annoy them.'

'And that *works*?'

'That's what the Sami told me. But that was brown bears. Black bears – you only get them in North America and they like to make the point that they're different to their sissy Old World cousins.'

'How?' Tikaani asked suspiciously.

'Well, they're less likely to attack in the first place – but if they do, it's probably because they're hungry and they won't be interested in you playing dead. And they can out-run you . . .'

'And out-climb me and out-swim me, I got that bit . . .'

'. . . So you just have to fight.'

'Fight,' Tikaani said flatly. 'I'm not exactly tall. Me, versus a huge bear?'

'Act aggressive,' Beck told him. 'Remember, it's dominance again. You wave your pack or your coat at it, if you have time to get them off. If you don't, then you jump up and down, you shout, you wave your arms.' He held his arms above his head and lunged at Tikaani. '*Raah!* You have to show it you're not a push-over – it's not worth its while to try and eat you.'

'No, it wouldn't be,' Tikaani agreed. 'I bet I taste really, really bad and I'd make sure I told them so.'

Beck laughed. 'Just don't give them the chance to find out!'

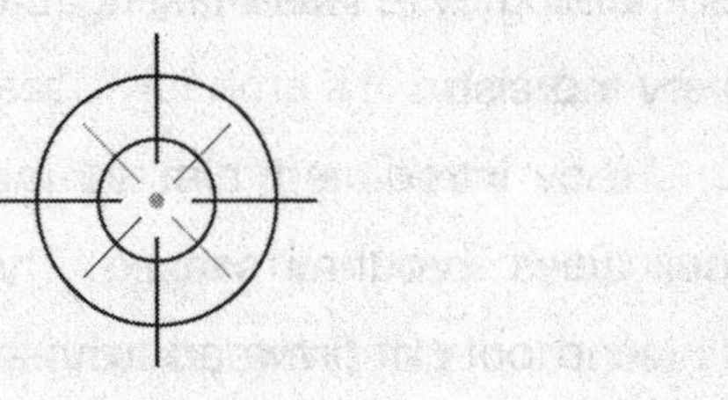

CHAPTER 13

But as the day drew on, they didn't see any bears at all. Beck made sure they drank from their water supply and ate a little at reasonable intervals, as well as gathering up any berries and mushrooms they passed to carry with them. There was no point in pressing on so fast that they wore themselves out.

'We're not going to get three regular meals a day,' he explained. 'We just graze as we go.'

Tikaani already knew a lot of the plants, thanks to his grandmother's teaching. Like the blueberries, which were not easy to find because they grew amongst other plants low down on the ground. The berries were tiny and quivered beneath the fingers at the slightest pressure. If they burst, which was almost inevitable, they stained the fingers with something like sweet-tasting blue ink. They were very moreish.

Beck introduced him to more of the natural delicacies that they passed. There were the pink-tinted shoots of fireweed, whose name came from the colour of its leaves but suited the strong taste perfectly. And coltsfoot, flat green leaves shaped like the ace of spades that they picked straight off the ground.

And then there were plants which neither of the boys could identify for sure. They gathered up likely-looking candidates to test later.

'So that's it,' Tikaani said flatly when Beck offered him some of the coltsfoot. 'We're officially eating plants.'

Beck looked at him sideways. 'Berries are plants and you ate those,' he said mildly.

'True,' Tikaani conceded with a smile. He nibbled at his leaf and his eyebrows went up. 'OK, it's not bad.' He looked thoughtful. 'And it was good enough for my ancestors to stay alive long enough to produce me, so maybe I ought to show it a bit more respect.'

Beck laughed as they set off again. 'Maybe they should put that on the packaging. "It kept your ancestors alive!"'

Tikaani fell into step beside him. 'My granddad would add, "So why are you buying it in a shop?"'

'So he's not totally in favour of the march of progress?' Beck asked wryly.

'Not . . . totally.' Tikaani put in just enough of a pause to emphasize the understatement. He pulled a face. 'Shops aren't *traditional*. I mean, I do know that food doesn't grow in supermarkets, right? Everything you find plastic-wrapped or in a tin used to grow in the soil, with dirt and bacteria and stuff. You buy a packet of minced beef and that means a cow died somewhere, with a lot of blood and gore. That's how it goes. I just don't see the big deal about doing it all yourself.'

He grinned. 'I remember once I didn't want to eat something, and he told me, "Your Uncle Kavik risked his life for this food!" and I was, like, "Well, I wish he wouldn't," and I got a clipped ear and sent to bed, so it went to waste and Uncle Kavik risked his life for nothing . . .'

Tikaani sighed. 'The thing is, if you grow your food on a farm, let someone else do all the catching and cleaning and preparing, and you buy it in a shop, no one has to risk their life and you've got time to do other stuff.'

'Such as?' Beck asked.

Tikaani chuckled, but there was a sour edge to it. 'OK, now we move on to my dad. I get on well with him, yeah, but he's all, "Why do you spend all your time with that computer? Why not get out more?"'

Beck kept quiet. He could sense a frustration in his companion that was bubbling to the surface in the form of words. Tikaani needed to let it out.

'I mean,' Tikaani went on, 'you're the first foreign friend I've met face to face, right? But you're not my first foreign friend ever. I've got several that I only know over the web. We can chat and hang together – we get on really well . . . and we're in different countries. The world is a huge place and I like to be part of it. How big is Anakat compared to the world? Anakat has a couple of hundred people but I'm part of a culture of millions. You need technology for that which Anakat just doesn't have.'

He clenched his fists and Beck sensed this was the final outburst: 'This is the modern world! You need technology!'

They walked in silence for a while after that. Beck thought of the GPS in his pocket. He hadn't used it lately because he knew how low the power was. He agreed with everything Tikaani said but with one addition: sooner or later, technology lets you down . . .

Fortunately, navigating wasn't hard. Beck had walked across plains and deserts before, where you fixed your eyes on a point on the horizon and headed for it. Here in the trees you couldn't see the horizon but you could see the mountains above them. The storm that had diverted the plane was long gone. The sharp, rocky peaks shone with gleaming coats of white snow, stark against the clear blue sky. They were beautiful, but Beck was very glad there was a pass that led through them.

Another few hours, he knew from the map, and they would reach a river. After that they would be in the foothills and then it would be time to rest for the night.

And apart from that clawed tree, there had been no sign of bears, or indeed any other kind of mammals . . .

Something moved in Beck's peripheral vision. He stopped dead and his head snapped round. Tikaani took a few steps forward before realizing that Beck wasn't keeping up.

'Hey? What's the problem?'

'Nothing . . .' Beck murmured. He peered into the trees.

Tikaani was back by his side in a flash. 'Bear?' he asked. He took a firmer grip on his stick and Beck could hear him making his tone brave.

'No,' Beck said firmly. 'Not a bear. Come on.'

He set off again and, after a moment, Tikaani caught up.

It had definitely not been a bear. If he had seen anything at all, it had been a sleek shadow, low to the ground, cruising just out of sight through the trees. It moved at the same pace as they did and was in no hurry to go anywhere.

He had seen similar behaviour in his time with the Sami. He knew exactly which animal acted like this. Stalking, in no hurry, waiting for reinforcements.

Beck bit his lip, held his own stick more firmly and decided not to worry Tikaani with it. But he was pretty certain they were being followed by a wolf.

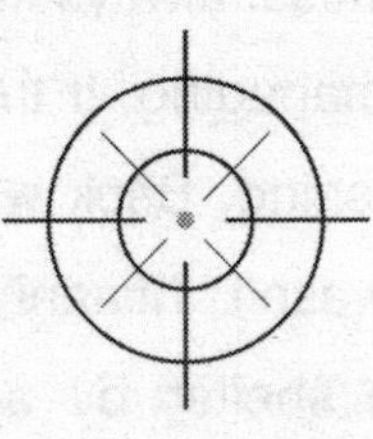

CHAPTER 14

Beck stood on the river bank and stared across in dismay.

Crystal-clear water came down from the mountains and flowed over a bed of stone and gravel. It didn't look that fast. In fact, it looked quite inviting. The water rippled and sun sparkled off the wavelets.

The river was only about fifty metres wide. He thought it might as well have been fifty miles. A branch swept by, turning slowly in the torrent. It shot past Beck at the speed of the average cyclist.

Beck clenched one fist, then the other, and then hit himself on both sides of the head at once. '*Duh!*'

They had made good progress. Not a sign of any bears, and even the wolf shape hadn't shown itself again. Beck had set up a brisk but steady pace through the wilderness, always keeping one eye on how Tikaani was managing. If the other boy found the pace too punishing, Beck was prepared to let up . . . a little. It wasn't Tikaani's uncle who was slowly dying in a shelter by a rock, waiting for rescue. But Tikaani, once he had found his stride, had kept up all the way.

And then this. Beck stared in frustration at the river, and bit his lip, and then kicked a nearby stone.

'Hey.' Tikaani looked at him sideways. 'You knew the river was here, right?'

'Yeah, I knew,' Beck said dully. 'The map and the GPS both have it.'

'And . . . ?'

'They don't show how big it is. I was really hoping for something smaller . . . and if it wasn't spring, it would be.'

The river was swollen with meltwater from the mountains. During the winter it would be frozen. During the summer it would be an idly trickling stream. Right here, right now, it was the biggest it got all year.

And it was going to be much harder to cross than

he had expected. It wasn't exactly a raging torrent. It wasn't foaming white water. But there was still so much of it. Calm, implacable and ready to sweep unwary travellers away at a moment's notice.

'So . . .' Tikaani raised an eyebrow at the river. 'We go along it?'

'I wish.' Beck scowled at the water. 'Yes, if we were lost, then following the river would be exactly right. Rivers go somewhere. You find towns and people if you follow them.'

'But,' Tikaani pointed out, 'we're not lost.'

'Nope.' Beck agreed. 'We know exactly where we are.' He took out the GPS and reached into his pants.

Tikaani looked on, frowning in puzzlement. 'And rummaging in our underpants will help us *how* exactly?' he demanded.

Beck grinned and showed his friend the batteries he'd retrieved. 'These need to be kept warm,' he explained. 'The colder they are, the quicker they lose their juice, you see.' He slotted the batteries into place, switched on the GPS and examined the screen. 'This river cuts along the foot of the mountains for miles before it heads for the sea,' he remarked. 'If we followed it until we got somewhere, it would take us so long that we might as well just go back to Uncle Al and wait.'

'So we . . . what? Wade?' asked Tikaani.

''S right,' Beck confirmed as he disassembled the GPS again. He walked right down to the water's edge and paced slowly along it, hands on hips. His scowl swept up and down the river. He wanted exactly the right spot. 'We wade.'

'Hey!' Tikaani yelped. 'I was joking!'

'Unfortunately, I wasn't . . .'

With a gentler river, Beck thought, he might have tried to build a raft. But even if he did build one now, it would just be swept away in the current. Wading was the only answer. Beck could already see it would be more than a paddle. Rolling their trousers up to their knees and just walking across didn't quite cover it.

'So . . .' Tikaani watched him pace along the bank. 'Exactly what are you doing now?'

'Looking for somewhere to cross.'

It was going to be touch and go – something

Beck *didn't* say out loud. Cold water took your strength – and there was the danger of underwater obstacles . . . They should give themselves the advantage of finding the best place to cross.

But it didn't take long for Beck to conclude that every point on the bank had pluses and minuses that cancelled each other out. He could choose a nice narrow bit, but there the current was strong and the water came thundering through. Then again, he could choose a wider bit where the current was gentler, but it would take longer to cross. He didn't want to go too far up- or downstream because that would just take them off course.

Finally Beck sat down on a rock and started to unlace his boots. 'We'll do it from here,' he announced. 'I'll go first. Make sure the way's safe.'

''Kay,' Tikaani grumbled. 'And if you get swept away I'll dive in and make sure you don't end up as seal food floating out to sea.'

Beck shrugged, then grinned. 'Or just go another way?'

First he took off all the clothes he could spare and thrust them into his rucksack. He made a protesting Tikaani do the same, though with just one layer on it was suddenly a lot colder. They each kept on a shirt and their trousers. It wouldn't keep them warm or dry, but it would be protection if the current threw them against a stone. Beck also put his sockless feet back into his boots and relaced them. The last thing he needed was to gash a foot or twist an ankle.

'And trust me,' he said as he tied the last knot, smiling up at Tikaani's sour face. 'Putting on dry socks after this will be the best feeling *ever*.'

They wrapped their rucksacks up in their coats for waterproofing, and used their home-made ropes to tie off the arms and the open ends. Finally Beck showed Tikaani how to hoist his rucksack right up and tie it so that it hung behind his neck, not at his waist as it usually did. Last of all he did the same for himself.

'Here goes nothing,' he said, forcing a smile for Tikaani's benefit. And he turned and walked into the river.

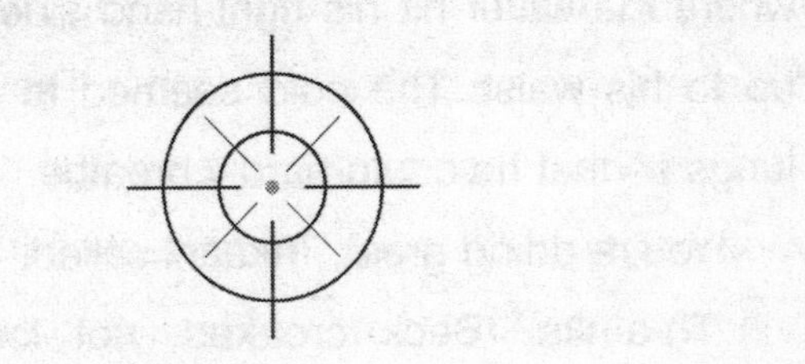

CHAPTER 15

With the first step, his feet merely felt cold. Then there was a trickle into his boots, followed a half-second later by a flood of ice-cold water. He winced, but kept walking. Then the water was right over his boots and working its way up to his knees.

The cold ate into him like an army of ants gnawing on his bones. Even though this was meltwater, which meant it was warmer than ice, it was still freezing. The force of the river was like an invisible noose around his ankles, trying to pull them from under him.

He made sure he was side-on to the current, offering the least resistance to the water, and checking for approaching hazards like logs. The river flowed from his right to his left, so the bow wave where the water hit his right-hand side was almost up to his waist. The cold seemed to paralyse his lungs so that he could hardly breathe.

'You're doing great,' Tikaani called.

'Th-a-nks,' Beck croaked, not looking back. 'Never better.'

That time in Colombia, he and his friends had forded a river. They had used vines from the jungle as support ropes so that no one would be swept away. But there were no vines here and the home-made ropes tying up the rucksacks weren't long enough. If the current caught him, there would be no fighting it.

And so every step had to be carefully planned. He could feel the water-smoothed rocks shift beneath his feet. At least with two legs and one stick he had three anchor points under the water to hold him steady. He always made sure that two were firm before moving the third. Every time he moved a numb foot forward he had to make sure it was planted on solid ground before he put his weight on it.

He knew he had about ten minutes before

hypothermia set in: his body would be losing heat faster than it was making it. Right now, every part of his body wanted to turn round and run back to Tikaani. But that would achieve nothing, except that he would be cold, wet and still on the wrong side. There was no point in losing all that body heat for nothing.

So, ten minutes to get across this torrent . . .

The cold was chewing its way up his body. It had reached his hips, his stomach, his ribs. Breathing was actively painful now. He had to force each gasp in and out of his lungs – *huh! huh! huh!* The deeper he went, the more of his body there was for the current to work on.

The water was now up to his armpits. He held his elbows out and tilted his head back to keep his chin dry. He could feel his rucksack bobbing madly against the back of his head. He hoped it would be staying dry in its waterproof wrapping.

Now the biting chill had gone – his body was just numb, apart from an ache deep inside his bones. There was so little feeling that it took a few more steps to realize – *the water was going down!*

Beck glanced down to confirm it. Yes, with each step the water level was dropping a little further down his chest. He was past halfway. Relief surged through him. He could do this.

Then a traitorous stone turned beneath his foot and his legs were swept away. The water closed over his head and he was swept tumbling away in a roaring torrent of ice.

Beck reacted without thinking and jammed his stick down into the river bed. It gave him a second's grace to find his footing again and he stood up. His head broke the surface, back into light and air, and he whooped for breath as water streamed down his face.

'Beck! Beck!'

Tikaani was running down the bank to follow him. In just that couple of seconds, Beck had travelled a long way downstream.

'I'm OK,' he gasped. Soaked, he thought, but OK. He wiped the hair out of his eyes and turned away from Tikaani to see how far he had to go. In fact the current had done him a favour and swept him a little closer to the far bank. He could feel the cold setting in from below and above. He just hoped his rucksack had survived its dunking because life was going to get so much more interesting if it hadn't and everything inside was wet.

The adrenaline surge from his accident gave him new strength to press on. Two minutes later the water was down to his knees. Then he was splashing through the shallows and finally he was out on the other side.

He longed to throw himself down on the ground and rest, but that way he would just freeze quietly. He had to keep moving. He whirled his arms round and round to force the blood back into his hands, which would warm him up fast.

'OK!' he called to Tikaani, hopping up and down. 'Your turn. Watch out for . . .' He paused, his attention caught by a standing wave in the water another twenty metres downstream. The river seemed to rise up a small ramp that stayed motionless in the water. From this angle the sun shone on it and he could see it clearly. From the other side of the river it had been just the same colour as the rest of water and he hadn't noticed it.

'Tikaani, come down here,' he called. If there was a standing wave, it meant the current was coming up against something on the river bed. There might well be a ridge of slightly higher ground at this point, which would mean the river would be shallower all the way across . . .

'This way,' he instructed, pointing. 'Use your stick for support, take each step carefully . . .'

A little less than ten minutes later, Tikaani had made his way across the river safely too. It had been a struggle against the current and the cold, but he had made it without being swept off his feet even once. By this time Beck was fully dressed in new, dry clothes – luckily, only a few drops of water had got into his rucksack. He had gathered wood and more Old Man's Beard for a fire and the first flame took hold even as Tikaani pulled on his own dry socks.

'Just like you said . . .' his friend noted, eyes closed in bliss. 'Best feeling ever.'

Beck grinned.

This wasn't to be their last stop of the day, but Beck knew they both needed the warmth of a fire more than anything else right now. They still had plenty of light left – this far north dark wouldn't fall until after eleven. They would spend a couple of hours here to thaw out, and then they would tackle the high ground.

He glanced up at the mountains that loomed above them.

Tikaani followed his gaze. 'It's all uphill from now on, isn't it?'

Beck nodded. The ground up to the far side of the river had been level and flat. Here it was already sloping up and away from them. The river really was the base of the mountains.

He hadn't seen the wolf again. It would be stranded the other side of the river now, anyway. But from now on they would be under increasing attack from other forces. Wind, ice, snow, cold – even gravity. A realm of no warmth and no food where it would be very easy to die without even realizing it.

'All uphill,' he agreed.

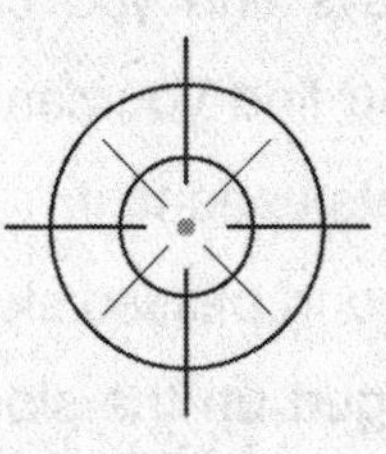

CHAPTER 16

They climbed for two more hours after leaving the river. They talked, but not much. It was more important to save their breath for walking. Beck kept an eye on his friend. He remembered how every muscle in his legs had been screaming the first time he climbed a mountain; that was probably how Tikaani was feeling now.

Beck showed him the way: put one foot in front of the other, maintain a steady rhythm and just keep going. Every hour you stopped for five minutes – which was enough to rest your limbs without allowing them to stiffen up. You needed mental discipline to get going again immediately the rest period was over.

'Just push through the pain barrier,' he urged his

friend. 'You'll always find you can take one more step. And then you find you can take another. And then your body gets used to it.'

And so the ground passed slowly in front of their eyes as they trudged up the side of the mountain. The cold wind, which just on its own could cause frostbite, was behind them and their rucksacks helped absorb its attack. But Beck remembered a figure he had been taught once – for every hundred metres you go up, the temperature drops by two degrees Celsius. By that reckoning they would be at freezing point before they reached the top of the mountains – which was why the peaks were clad in snow and ice.

It also meant that once they were heading downhill again, the temperature would go *up* two degrees for every hundred metres of descent. That was something to look forward to.

Beck wondered about making a noise to scare off any bears, but as the trees thinned out it seemed less important. He couldn't believe any bears would be hanging around up here when there would be so much more for them down on the plain. Animals have a big advantage over humans, he thought ruefully; they know where they're better off and they stay there.

Finally he decided it was time to call a halt for the day.

'This'll do,' he said. The non-stop uphill terrain had actually dipped a little and the ground was flat. They were among the very last of the trees. Above them was just rock, with a very thin covering of soil. And soon after that, just snow and ice.

To mark the spot he ceremonially undid his rucksack clips and let it fall to the ground behind him. Tikaani did likewise.

'Thank you,' his friend said earnestly, then took a few steps to ease his aching legs. 'I really couldn't have taken— *Wow!*'

Tikaani had looked back the way they had come. Beck came to stand beside him and together they looked proudly out over Alaska.

Beck estimated they had climbed a good thousand metres since they had crossed the river. Below them, trees and tundra merged together into a patchwork quilt flung all the way to the horizon, where it merged into a grey sky. Maybe they had been higher than this in the plane, but when you were up there you felt cut off from the scene. Now, standing on the ground, the two boys actually felt part of this astonishing landscape.

'We did all that today?' Tikaani asked, amazed. '*We* did *that*?'

'Yup,' Beck agreed. 'We did that.'

He looked out at the incredible vista with less enthusiasm. Normally he would have loved to enjoy the view. But somewhere down there was Uncle Al in his makeshift shelter, and he wasn't getting any better. So while Tikaani looked at the tundra far below, and marvelled at the awesome beauty, Beck thought of it as one third of their journey. With two thirds still to come.

He patted Tikaani on the shoulder. 'Come on – we need to make a shelter while it's still light.'

He looked around, considering. Ideally he would have liked to make an A-frame shelter, like the one he had built in Colombia for himself, Marco and Christina. It would be sturdy and give the best protection against the elements. But it would need good strong branches cut off a tree, and he only had the Bowie knife, not a saw.

'We'll make a lean-to,' he decided, 'and we'll make it here.'

He stood between a pine tree and a boulder that came up to his shoulders. At about the same height on the tree there was a fork in the branches. 'We need to find a branch that's good and straight.' He tapped the fork, then the rock. 'We put it across here, and lean other branches and stuff against it. It'll block out the wind and we can sleep in its shelter.'

'There's still one side open,' Tikaani pointed out.

'Yup. The fire goes that side. Trust me – we'll be snug as a bug in a rug.'

'Any bugs in my rug,' Tikaani muttered, 'get squished.'

They soon found the main branch for the shelter, still attached to a tree nearby. The wood was too thick to cut with the knife, but by hanging on it with their combined weight they made it sheer off until it was only attached by a few strands which the knife could handle. They laid it across from the fork in the tree to the rock, and started to look for other branches on the ground that they could prop against it.

'What do we do tomorrow?' Tikaani asked as they searched. He jerked a thumb upwards, pointing up the mountain. 'No trees up there.'

'We're not going to spend a night in the snow,' Beck promised. 'Not if I can help it. This time tomorrow we'll be up and over and down in the trees on the other side of the mountain. So we'll probably do the same again. OK, we need foliage – plenty of it. If it's going to be windproof, we want it at least ten centimetres thick . . .'

'OK,' Tikaani said. 'I think I saw some loose branches over here . . .'

He ducked behind some trees, out of sight for a moment. Beck decided he would start gathering wood for a fire. There were plenty of dry, dead twigs that could be used for kindling, and he crouched down to scoop up a handful.

'*Beck! Beck!*'

Beck jumped to his feet as Tikaani burst back through the trees. The two boys almost collided.

'Beck!' Tikaani grabbed hold of him, effectively pinning his arms to his side. 'It's a bear! I think it's a bear. It was brown and . . . *it's a bear!*'

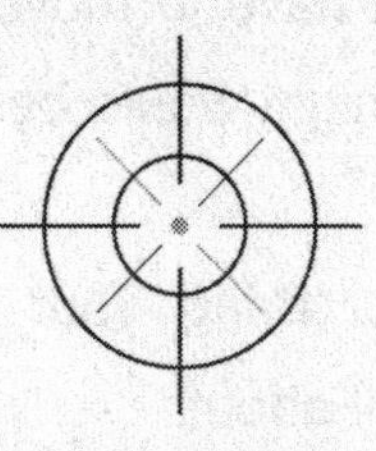

CHAPTER 17

Beck's heart plummeted. A bear? He had been so sure they were out of bear territory. Their little shelter wouldn't stand up to an inquisitive bear for a second. If they had to sleep with bears around, then one of them would have to stand watch while the other slept – but they both needed a good night's rest.

'Brown?' he asked, carefully working himself free of Tikaani's grip. 'Not black?'

'Um . . .' Tikaani swallowed. His face was pale and he was sweating. 'Yeah. I think so. I . . . uh . . .'

Good, Beck thought. At least there would be a chance of scaring it off. But black . . . black bears attacked. If it was a black bear, they would have no choice. They would have to scare it off and move on before it summoned up the courage to come after them. They would have to move up into the snow and ice and their night would be a lot less comfortable.

'OK,' he said. 'Bring your rucksack and be prepared to wave it about.'

'What?' Tikaani looked at him like he was mad. 'We're going looking for it?'

'Maybe we can drive it off. We can't let it hang around. It's got all the mountains to spend the night in – we need to do it here.' Beck took a firm grip on the knife with one hand and held a stick in the other. 'And start shouting.'

'W-what should I shout?'

'Something. Anything! Sing a song!'

And so they pushed into the undergrowth as noisily as they could. Beck banged his knife against the stick and shouted out all the nursery rhymes he could remember. Tikaani gave a tuneless rendering of *America the Beautiful*.

'It was here,' Tikaani said a couple of minutes later. 'Just over there by those rocks . . .'

Beck pressed slowly forward. He glanced down at the ground . . .

. . . and burst out laughing. It was like a sudden sneeze that caught him unawares. He couldn't have kept it in if he'd tried. He didn't want Tikaani to think he was laughing at him so he tried to keep it quiet. He stood staring at the ground, slightly cross-eyed with the effort of smothering his laughter, and his shoulders shook.

'What?' Tikaani sounded cold at first. But then: 'Wha-at?' The laugh was infectious, spreading to the other boy in spite of himself. Tikaani probably realized that if Beck was just standing there giggling, then there wasn't any danger.

'Look.' Beck, still trembling, knelt down and poked the ground with his stick. There was a small pile of droppings and a line of footprints the size of cat paws heading away. Each one was divided in two.

Beck followed them with his eyes, and then pointed. A smaller pair of eyes was looking at them through the undergrowth about ten metres away. Their owner was about the size of a dog. It turned and fled in a flash of brown fur, speckled with white.

'It was a deer,' Beck said. The laugh was still

bubbling inside him. 'About as harmless as you can get.'

'A *deer*!' Tikaani exclaimed. 'I was frightened by a *deer*?'

'Well' – Beck poked the droppings – 'it might have been more frightened by you.'

Tikaani looked at the little pile, then up at Beck, and his own expression started to crumble. Then both boys burst out laughing again, and they laughed until they were sagging against each other.

Finally, still with the occasional snigger, they made their way back to the shelter and finished it off. Slim branches thick with pine needles, propped between the ground and the big horizontal branch, gave their shelter a windproof rear wall that they could huddle behind.

'Dinner time!' said Beck. 'A starter of berries, followed by berries and mushrooms, topped off by a dessert of berries. Let's see what we've got . . .'

As they had walked along, they had gathered food up and divided it between what they knew was safe and what only might be. The definitely safe food went into their left pockets, the 'maybe' food into the right. Now they turned out their pockets to make two piles.

'OK,' Beck said as they explored the second little heap. He poked the berries and leaves apart with his finger. 'Let's decide what's OK to eat . . .'

'What happens if it isn't but we still eat it?' Tikaani wanted to know.

'Symptoms may include anything from stomach pains and vomiting and diarrhoea, to death.' Beck said it conversationally, as if he was delivering aircraft safety instructions.

'OK, I'm all ears,' Tikaani agreed earnestly.

'Right. Anything with yellow or white berries – best avoid to be sure. Just chuck them out.' Beck flicked a couple of specimens to one side. 'Plants with shiny leaves, ditto . . .'

That helped them whittle the pile down.

'Next, smell them. If the smell is bitter or sort of almondy . . .'

'Chuck them,' Tikaani said happily, getting the idea. He put a leaf to his nose and breathed in thoughtfully.

That made the pile a little smaller still. Beck

looked at what was left. Ideally, testing food should take twenty-four hours or more. They couldn't really do that. He was only going to let them eat stuff he was as sure of as he could be. He picked out examples of different kinds of plant.

'Crush these,' he said, demonstrating, 'and rub the juice on the inside of your wrist, here, where it's tender. I'll do it with these ones here, you do it with those. Rub it on different places . . . if your skin becomes inflamed or you get a rash, we don't eat them. Give it five minutes.'

'What do we do for five minutes?'

Beck smiled and passed Tikaani a pile of the 'safe' berries. 'We eat the good ones!'

It wasn't much of a feast but it filled the empty holes inside them. None of the tested berries seemed to do them any harm either.

'On the whole, blue and black berries are usually OK,' Beck told Tikaani; 'red ones should always be approached with caution. And if you do eat anything that starts to make you feel sick,' he added, 'swallow charcoal from the fire. That'll bring it back up in an instant.'

'Oh, how I love living rough . . .' Tikaani murmured.

Now that they had a reasonable idea of what was safe to eat and what wasn't, they used the last half-hour of sunlight to search for more food – enough to get them over the mountains the next day and down into the trees on the other side.

And finally they could sleep. They lay back-to-back for warmth with their heads pillowed on the rucksacks and hats pulled down over their eyes. Judging by the sound of his breathing, Tikaani was asleep almost at once. The shelter was snug, as Beck had promised. The wind knocked against it from the other side, but none of it got through. The air inside the shelter was still, retaining its warmth, and the fire radiated heat. Beck lay on his side and listened to the wood crackling gently.

And then he thought of Uncle Al, alone in a shelter not much bigger than this. Had he kept his fire going? Did he still have any strength? How was he?

Suddenly Beck sat bolt upright. Two eyes

twinkled back at him from the dark. Beck's heart was pounding.

The eyes had gone but he could have sworn . . .

They had been close together, reflecting green in the light, the way dogs' eyes did. Or wolves'.

Were there wolves up here? He had been half asleep: maybe he was imagining it . . .

Beck lay cautiously back down and thought. There was no question of moving on now – if there were wolves out there, they would just follow them. And it had only been one pair of eyes; wolves hunted in packs, so there should have been many more.

Another predator? Maybe a wolverine? What colour were their eyes? He didn't know.

But wolves rarely attacked humans . . .

And the fire should keep any animals away . . .

And . . .

Beck fell asleep while he was still thinking through options.

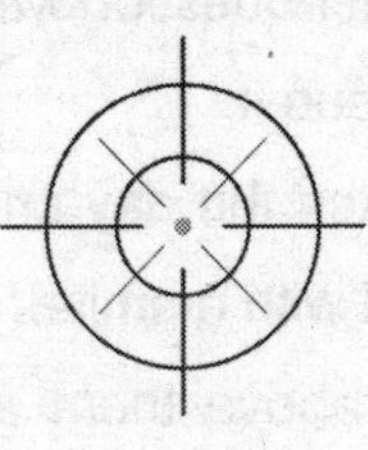

CHAPTER 18

'What are you looking for?' asked Tikaani.

Beck started; he hadn't realized Tikaani was awake.

It was the second day of their journey. He had woken with the sun, which he tended to do whenever he was sleeping out of doors. Then he had got up to check their little camp for signs of animal intrusion during the night. There were none – no scratches, no paw prints – and he had decided he'd just imagined the eyes last night. He had only seen them for a moment anyway.

'Just . . . checking,' he said.

Tikaani was sitting up in the shelter, rubbing his eyes sleepily. 'So does the maid bring us breakfast or do we have to get it ourselves?' he asked. It looked like his earlier question was already forgotten so Beck didn't pursue it.

'The maid's taken the day off. We have to get it ourselves,' he said with a smile. Then he looked up at the mountains above them and thought about what else they had to do that day. Cross the mountains; get across some thick, deep snow fields and down the other side.

'And if she isn't back by the time we've eaten,' he added, 'I'll have to ask you to give me a hand.'

'You know,' Tikaani said later, 'a pair of these from the store in Anakat would set you back, like, a hundred dollars.'

He was holding the two ends of a thin branch that Beck had broken off a tree. It was supple and evergreen, which meant it bent easily. Beck had forced the two ends round towards each other so that now it was shaped like the head of a tennis racket. He looked up from his work and grinned.

'I bet they wouldn't be tailor-made for the individual,' he pointed out.

'Well, no,' Tikaani agreed with a straight face. 'Craftsmanship of this quality can't be bought.'

Beck was making them each a pair of snow-shoes. They were going to be walking through snow later on. He knew there was nothing more tiring, and nothing more likely to give you frostbite. Tikaani knew all about frostbite. It was something else that you couldn't grow up in an Anak community and not be aware of. The body withdrew blood from your extremities – your ears, your nose, your toes and fingers – to conserve your core heat. It meant that ice crystals formed where the blood had been, splitting the cells open. The cells died and became infected. Ultimately a doctor would have to remove the dead limb to save your life.

No, they did not want frostbite.

While Tikaani held the two ends, Beck lashed them together with some of the wire from the plane. Next he took a rectangle of canvas that he had cut out of a shirt from the bags, and used more wire to tie it to the frame he had created. With the canvas in place he tied thin, sturdy sticks in place across the tennis racket. They strengthened the basic frame and would provide support for his foot when he came to put the snowshoe on.

With that done they repeated the procedure three more times so that each of them had a pair. Then they gathered up their things into their rucksacks, kicked earth over the campfire, and set off with the snowshoes tied to their backs.

It didn't take long to reach the snow. They left the trees behind and the ground grew hard beneath their feet. No more soft pine needles now; just dark, frozen earth with scraps of wiry, stubbly grass.

The first patch of snow was only about a metre across. It was draped like a sheet over a hummock of rocks. But these patches became more and more frequent, and closer and closer together, until eventually there was just snow and ice beneath their boots. It formed a very thin, frozen layer over dry, powdery snow beneath. With every step they took there was a little resistance, then a crunch beneath their feet as they broke through the crust.

'OK,' Beck decreed. He brushed the snow off a rock and sat down on it. 'Shoes on.'

He fastened Tikaani's first, then his own. He used more wire to fasten them around Tikaani's heels.

'They're going to feel a little weird at first. You might find they knock together as you walk. You just have to get used to that and take care. And from now on, while we're on the snow, keep wiggling your fingers and toes. Always. It keeps the blood flowing. Don't let it stop for a moment.'

'I know, I know.' Tikaani took a few experimental steps. 'Frostnip.'

'Right. It can get you in sixty seconds.'

Frostnip was the first stage of frostbite. It only affected the surface layers of the skin – but it was painful and the damaged cells never grew back.

'I will wiggle,' Tikaani promised. He waddled off across the snow in his snowshoes. 'I feel like a duck!'

Beck grinned. He could see his friend's point. 'Quack-quack!' he said, and then laughed and ducked as Tikaani threw a snowball at him.

But the air was too thin for much of that; they needed to keep their strength for walking. The snow and ice rose up around them as they headed towards the peaks. It was a pristine field of white.

Beck strained his eyes up ahead for any sign of the pass they were heading for, but he couldn't see it yet. Well, he told himself, they were still some distance away.

The ground undulated between rises and dips but always the average direction was up. Where it got too steep Beck told Tikaani to walk up the slope in zigzags, which gave them a shallower and easier rate of climb. The sun was still low in the sky – in fact it was about the same height above the horizon as they were – and their long shadows danced over the ice next to them.

After a while the ground levelled out again. It was a kind of plateau, halfway up the mountain. There was a cliff ahead with just a small gap in the middle that led on upwards. On their left, the cliff swept up to a sheer drop. On their right it merged with another cliff at right angles to the first.

The flat ground made the going easier.

'Keep your eyes open and watch out for snow that looks a little darker than the rest,' Beck said. 'And it might be sagging slightly too, like there's a slight dip beneath it.'

'OK . . .' Tikaani looked around. There wasn't anything like that yet. 'Only, the way you say that makes me think it won't actually be a slight dip.'

'Nope,' Beck agreed, 'it will be a huge one! At the moment there's still ground underneath us, but as we climb higher it'll be ice. And when there's ice beneath the snow, you get crevasses: huge great cracks in the ice that can kill you if you fall into—*STOP!*'

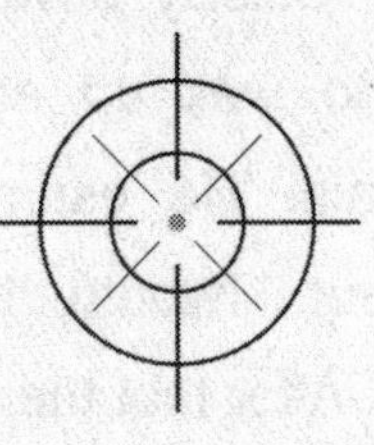

CHAPTER 19

Tikaani froze exactly where he was. Beck stared down at the ground in horror, then looked back the way they had come. Their footprints marched side by side across the smooth snow to where they were now.

The *too*-smooth snow. Beck looked around quickly and his heart sank. He had been looking out for crevasses and missed a danger that was just as great – and more immediate.

Experimentally he poked at the snow by his feet, scraping it away with his stick. The tip hit something hard, but it made a dull, flat noise. It wasn't scraping against rock.

'We're standing on ice,' he said quietly. 'There's a frozen lake under this lot.'

Tikaani looked quickly down at his feet, as if expecting water to well up around them. Beck looked back again. He estimated they hadn't come that far out. Twenty, twenty-five metres maybe – no more. After that the smooth snow tilted up and a black rock poked up. That would be solid ground.

'Turn round,' he said, 'and walk back over your own footprints . . .'

The ice they had already crossed was strong enough to take their weight. They turned round, and half a minute later were safely back on dry land.

Beck studied the smooth area in front of them with a lot more attention. Only a fool walked across frozen ice if there was a safer way round. The lake was a totally flat stretch of snow for about seventy metres. After that the ground started to slope up again.

He looked from side to side. They were boxed in by rock and by the sheer drop on their left. The lake was the only way forward, but one false step and they could be dunked in freezing water. If that happened, with the wind chill reducing the temperature even further, then hypothermia would follow as surely as night followed day.

'We don't have a choice,' he said reluctantly. 'We have to go that way . . .'

Beck led the way cautiously down to the edge of the lake and scraped the snow aside again with his stick. The ice beneath was grey and rough.

'The problem is,' he said, 'ice beneath snow is never going to be that thick. The snow insulates it and stops it from freezing further.'

'So we go straight over,' said Tikaani. 'Shortest distance, shortest time.'

'No, that's the thinnest ice,' Beck added. He rapped the grey ice a couple of times. It seemed solid, but it needed to be a good five centimetres thick, he knew, to hold their weight safely. Unfortunately there was no way of telling if it was. 'The lake will have frozen from the edges inwards, so the ice at the edge will be the oldest and thickest. We have to go round the edge.'

'You can tell me about how to test food,' Tikaani said, firmly. 'Let me tell you about ice. Look.' He pointed at the edge of the lake, the route Beck intended to take. It was a jumble of loose rocks that had fallen into the water. 'Rocks sticking up out of the ice mean the ice will be much thinner.'

Beck bit his lip. He could see Tikaani's point. Unfortunately he also knew that the ice in the middle of the lake could be paper-thin.

'So we compromise,' he said.

The boys made their way cautiously onto the lake and around the side, as close to the edge as seemed safe, but not too close to each other – they didn't want their combined weight putting pressure on any one point.

Tikaani was right – the ice around the rocks was thin. Beck could feel it flex beneath his feet. Halfway round, a large boulder jutted out from the edge, and to stay away from it they had to go out almost to the middle of the lake. With every step, Beck felt the ice creak beneath him. Any moment now he expected it to crack with a sound like a rifle shot and his foot to go through. They were still wearing their snowshoes, which spread the weight of their bodies, but still Beck felt the lake resented them. It knew they were foreign to these mountains; it didn't want them here.

But the far shore – the rocks and the rising slope that showed solid ground – was getting gradually closer. Beck didn't get ahead of himself. Even when the shore was only a couple of metres away, he scraped away the snow to check the ice before moving forward. Even if just his foot went through the thin ice at the edge, he could end up with frostbitten toes as ice formed inside his boot.

But finally he was standing on solid ground. He turned and beamed triumphantly at Tikaani. 'Made it!'

Tikaani smiled back, and took a step towards him.

Suddenly there was a snap that echoed off the rock face, and a splash, and Tikaani vanished as if he had fallen through a trap door.

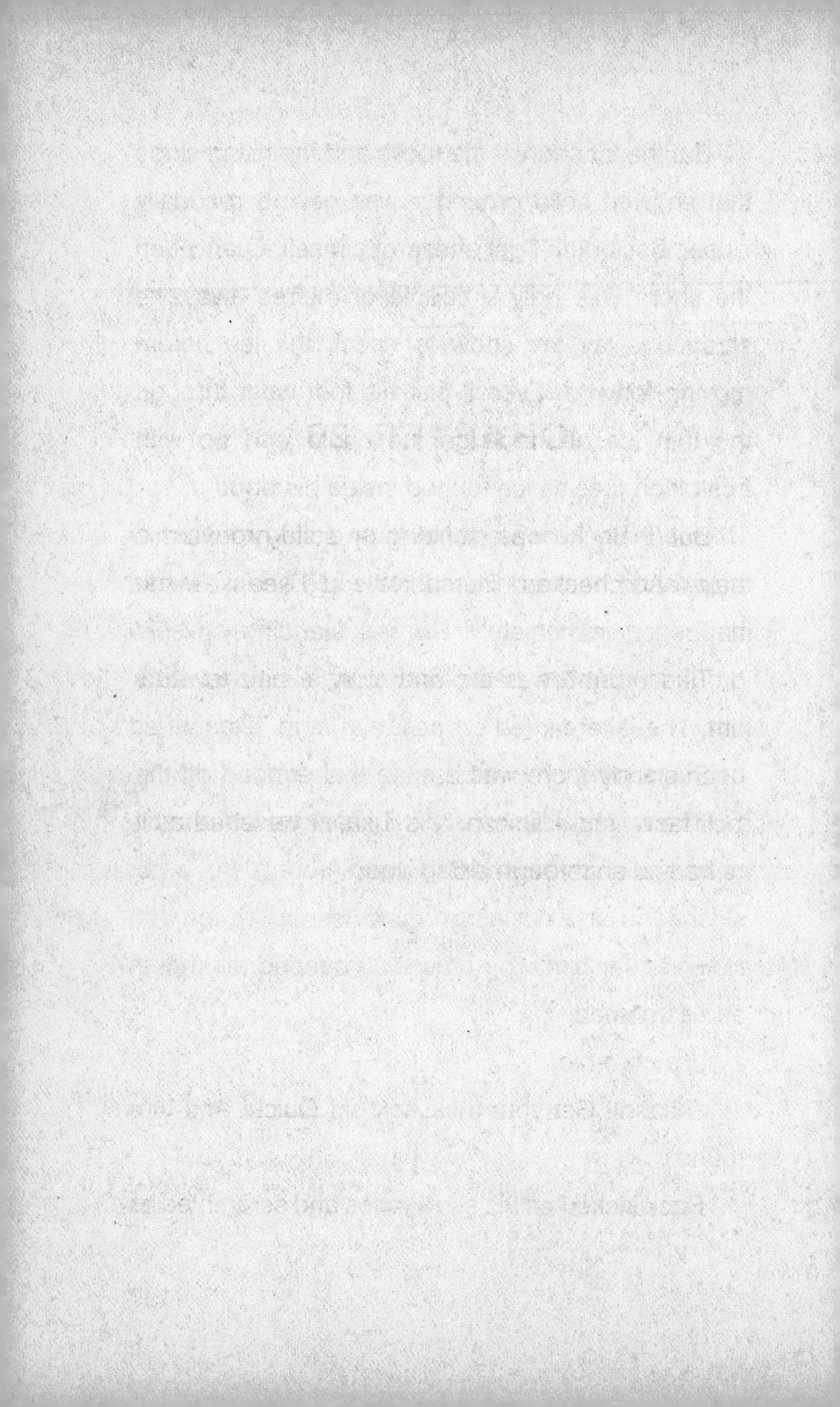

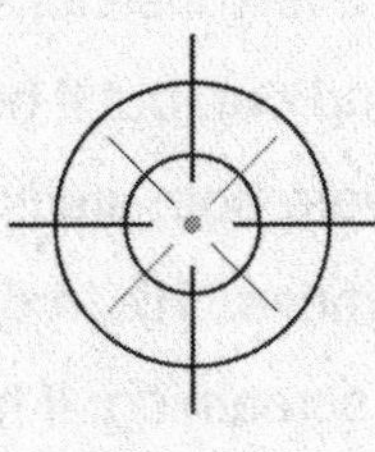

CHAPTER 20

'*Tikaani!*' Beck howled. He took a step forward to help, and checked himself. He could see what had happened immediately. He was standing on solid ground – but it was a promontory, a bit that stuck out. The lake carried on past him, and Tikaani had been standing on that bit.

The boy had flung out his arms as he fell, and his head and shoulders hadn't gone through. But water sloshed in and out of the dark hole in the ice and sluiced over him. The other boy opened his mouth and screamed.

'*It's co-o-old!*'

'Tikaani! Get your rucksack off! Quick! And turn round . . .'

Beck kicked off his snowshoes and scrambled as

close as he dared. Every instinct screamed at him to go and pull his friend out, but if he went through the ice too then they were both stuck.

Tikaani didn't move. His mouth was still wide open, as if he was screaming. If he was, it had risen to a pitch Beck couldn't hear. Now that the water had settled down, it was obvious that Tikaani was standing on the bottom of the lake. It was only about shoulder deep. That was a small bit of good news in a whole torrent of bad.

'*Tikaani!*' Beck shouted again.

Tikaani gaped at Beck, his breath coming in agonized pants.

'Tikaani. Ditch the rucksack and turn round. You know the ice is thick back there. It'll help you climb out . . .'

Tikaani's breaths were coming faster and faster. Beck could picture what was happening inside him. In many cases, the gasp reflex of the shock of freezing water made people breathe water into their lungs. At least Tikaani hadn't done that yet. But hypothermia could set in within minutes. There was the all-consuming, mind-numbing effect of the cold. The body would lose sensation; all Tikaani's coordination and strength would freeze at the bottom of the lake. And if he wasn't quick, there was the risk of cardiac arrest – a heart attack, brought on by the shock.

'Turn round,' Beck said again loudly. Tikaani would be losing the ability to concentrate, to coordinate his movements. He had to be handled firmly. '*Turn round*.'

Tikaani began to turn. His fingers fumbled at the buckle of his rucksack and it fell away, bobbing in the water. Beck quickly snagged it with his stick before it could sink. 'Good, good. Now pass me your snowshoes.'

Tikaani somehow managed to pull the snowshoes off his feet and throw them towards Beck.

'That's it! Now climb out – go on, climb out!' Beck instructed.

Tikaani managed to prop his elbows on the ice and work his way forward. Soon his top half was free of the water, then his waist and his thighs. He crawled painfully forward until at last he was out of the lake. Already his sodden trousers seemed to be hardening in the cold.

'Here!' Beck called. 'Over here! Quick!'

Tikaani crawled over to Beck's promontory, and Beck reached out and pulled him to safety on solid ground. Tikaani's face was contorted in agony. His arms were clenched to his sides and already his body shook in huge, muscle-wrenching shivers.

'*Co-o-old!*' he groaned.

''S OK . . . you're safe now . . . come on . . .' Beck clutched his friend and held him up as they stumbled away from the ice.

'*Cold!*'

'Yeah, I know. Come on, we'll get you warm . . .'

Beck bit his lip, and looked around the snowy waste. Get him warm? How?

But he had to do it, because if he didn't, then in just a few minutes Tikaani would be dead.

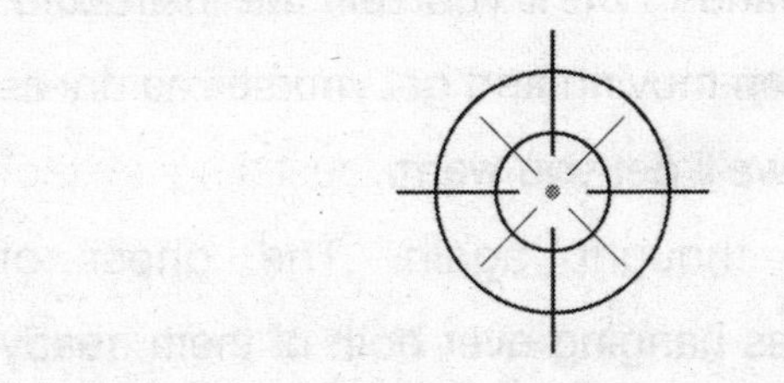

CHAPTER 21

'Tikaani, strip!'

Tikaani's whole body vibrated with shivers and his face was contorted with pain, but his eyes went round with surprise.

'Do it!' Beck snapped.

'Gee . . .' Tikaani muttered, fumbling with numb, shaking fingers at his buttons. 'D-d-didn't know it . . . w-was that . . . k-kind of holiday . . .'

'*All* your clothes,' Beck said when Tikaani was down to his shorts.

Tikaani reluctantly obeyed. 'OK,' he said. His goose-pimpled flesh was rough as sandpaper. 'Now w-w-what?'

But Beck had already started rubbing him dry with a T-shirt from his pack. He pushed the T-shirt into Tikaani's hands. 'Do it yourself,' he instructed. 'You have to keep moving and get yourself as dry as you can. Then we'll get you warm.'

Warm! he thought again. The ghost of hypothermia was hanging over both of them, ready to pounce; ready to freeze them, turn their blood into ice, make them one with the snowy wastes. To survive, the body slowly shut itself down, focusing more and more effort on keeping the vital organs warm and alive. Finding an external source of warmth was the only treatment.

Beck snatched up his rucksack – there would be nothing dry in Tikaani's – and began to rummage through it. A trickle of sweat ran down his forehead and immediately he forced himself to slow down. This was the most important thing he had ever done – he had never had a friend so close to dying before – and he *had to slow down*. If he started sweating, then that damp sweat would eventually freeze – and then the hypothermia would pounce and they would be dead together.

OK, good. There were dry clothes in here that Tikaani could wear. His boots were still soaking wet

– there was nothing to be done about that – but Tikaani would be dry again. That all-important layer of warm air would form next to his skin. His body would keep its heat.

For the time being, anyway. But he was still deeply chilled.

'OK,' Beck said. He scraped snow off a rock and left the clothes piled on top of it. 'Put these on.'

And now came the biggest challenge. He stood up straight and looked around, hands on his hips. He had to make a fire. By themselves, clothes wouldn't do the trick for someone who had just been immersed in freezing water. Tikaani needed an extra source of heat. He needed a fire.

A fire? Up here?

Beck's gaze roamed over the snow and ice. The nearest trees were a couple of hours' walk away, downhill. What was he going to do? Burn rocks?

His mind went, reluctantly, to the contents of his rucksack. OK. The rest of their clothes would burn. The makeshift ropes they had fashioned back at the plane would burn. But they wouldn't burn for long enough, and anyway, he *so* didn't want to do that . . .

'Hey, Tikaani. Are the mountains snow-covered all year at this height?'

Tikaani scowled up at him as he pulled on the trousers. 'Yes. No. Well, the tops are but the lower bits are clear in the summer. Why?'

Beck was pleased to see that the violent shaking had already died down. A little. His friend's body still shivered.

'Because if this area is clear during the summer, there might be . . .'

He looked around again. If any plants grew up here at all, under the snow, they would be in sheltered places. He crouched down beside a boulder and burrowed into the snow with his hands.

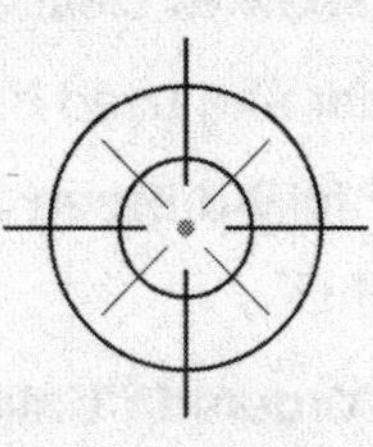

CHAPTER 22

Yes! Beck's fingers closed around something hard and round. He brushed away the snow. Dark, twisted wood: some kind of bush that was waiting for summer's thaw to put out new shoots. He wrapped his fingers around it and tore it up from the earth, then scrabbled through the snow around it, clearing away more potential fuel. He snapped one of the twigs and it broke with a very satisfactory *crack*. It glistened with flakes that melted in his hand. It had spent the winter under the snow, but inside it was dry.

Beck used the knife to fluff up the bark, exposing the dry wood inside so that the twigs would catch fire more easily. For kindling he used bits of cotton wool that he'd taken from the plane's first aid kit. He kicked aside more snow to clear a patch of ground in the lee of a boulder and used his fire iron to strike the first sparks. A fully-dressed Tikaani crouched down beside him.

'No way,' Beck ordered. 'Until this fire's going, you walk.'

Tikaani looked up at him. 'I what? Where?'

'You walk. Round and round in circles if you have to. Make your body generate its own warmth. Your core's frozen – you have to give it a hand. Go on! Walk! And bring your knees up high with each step.'

Tikaani glared at him with something like hate, but he slowly began to walk round and round the fire, rubbing himself, while Beck coaxed a flame up out of the cotton wool and a few lengths of cloth that he'd cut from his home-made rope with the Bowie knife.

'And don't rub your arms like that,' he said absently, concentration still fixed on the fire. 'It draws blood away from your body core and cools you down. Wave your arms around fast instead. That will force blood into your hands and warm you up. It works, I promise.'

Tikaani stopped, glared at him, and started walking again. He wheeled his arms around as he walked now.

'Once there was this guy called Ernest Shackleton,' Beck told him as he trudged. 'Went on an expedition to the South Pole before the First World War.'

He knelt and blew gently onto the fire. A tiny lick of flame was spreading across the rope. As it went, it grew. Beck finished his story:

'One of his crew fell into the water there. They were on an ice floe – nothing to burn at all. He just had to walk round and round the floe for twelve hours. Just walk, and walk, and walk, until eventually he was dry. *Twelve hours!* But it kept him alive. No one died. They all came home again.'

The fire was taking. The flame seemed to rub shyly against the wood, as if it really wanted it to join in the fun. The wood didn't seem to know quite what to make of it. It had been expecting a few more weeks beneath the snow before it emerged into the world again for the summer. But it let itself be persuaded. The curls of bark began to join in with the kindling. A wisp of smoke rose up into the mountain air.

Beck continued to blow until he was *absolutely* sure. It wasn't a fluke; it wasn't just going to burn out in a couple of minutes. Then he sat back on his haunches and sighed with relief.

'OK – come and sit down, Tikaani,' he said, while he stood up to search for more wood. Immediately Tikaani was on the other side of the fire, crouching down, holding out his hands to absorb the heat. This was never going to be a raging bonfire but it tipped the balance. Tikaani would live.

Beck grinned in sheer relief. Tikaani smiled back.

'Hold your feet out as well,' Beck suggested. 'You can warm up from both directions . . .'

There was more fuel like the first load, buried under snow in drifts around rocks. Beck gathered as much as he could find. Then, while Tikaani thawed out, Beck stuffed his boots with more cut-off lengths of rope. They were going to be walking through ice and snow; damp boots would just suck the warmth straight out of Tikaani's feet, asking for frostbite. Beck held them out, upside down, over the fire so that the warm air could add to the drying out.

'I think I can do that,' Tikaani said. He took the boots off Beck and held them out to dry himself. His voice was fully back to normal – no chattering teeth, no bouts of shivering. 'I do have other skills apart from falling into water.'

'Of course you do,' Beck agreed with a smile. 'That's world-class holding, that is.'

Tikaani looked abashed. 'I've held us up, haven't I? I mean, you wanted to press on, get over the top before sunset.'

'Hey, we still can.' Beck glanced up at the peak. 'OK, we've lost a couple of hours, but it stays light late. So we'll just be walking a bit longer, that's all.'

'Yeah. But I'm sorry.'

'No worries.' Beck bit his lip. 'It could have happened to me too.' He added, half to Tikaani and half to himself: 'I should have noticed the lake didn't end there. I need to be more careful.'

He stood up, more to end the conversation than anything else. He didn't want to dwell on this but he had to face up to it. It had been one small mistake, but they were in a land that didn't tolerate any mistakes at all. Beck resolved there and then that he wouldn't be making any more.

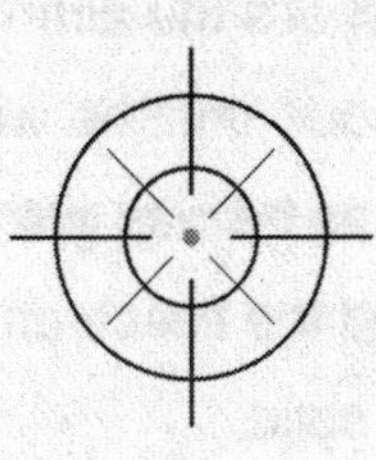

CHAPTER 23

Beck tipped out the contents of Tikaani's sodden rucksack to see if anything was still dry. It was a forlorn hope. The wet rope probably didn't matter; the wet clothes very well could.

And then there were the clothes Tikaani had been wearing, which were soaked through. The water brushed off the coat easily, so at least he still had that, but he could do with a fleece as well, and they didn't have a spare that was dry.

Beck wrung out the fleece until as much of the water was gone as possible. Then he spread it out on a rock along with the other items and went back to the fire.

'I don't know if they're going to dry there, or just freeze,' Tikaani said.

Beck grinned. 'That's the aim!'

He gave it an hour, until he was certain Tikaani was as warmed up as he was going to get. Then he stood up and peeled the fleece off the rock. It was a sheet of ice, frozen solid.

Beck folded it so that the ice snapped and cracked in his hands, and whacked it hard against the rock. He closed his eyes as bits of ice flew everywhere. He did this a couple more times, then shook the fleece out again for Tikaani to see.

'It's almost completely dry!' Tikaani exclaimed. He ran his fingers over it to check. 'That's amazing.'

Beck bit back a grin. For a moment his friend reminded him of a housewife in a TV ad plugging a new cleaning product.

'New Improved DryClothes, TM,' he said, putting on the smooth and insincere tones of a TV announcer.

'Now With Added Dryness!' Tikaani added. 'So . . . it froze, right?'

'Yup,' Beck agreed, 'and once all the water is frozen, you can just bash it out.'

He gathered up the other clothes he had put out.

They were icy but they hadn't completely dried yet. 'OK. Once we've got a shelter for the night we'll leave these out and they'll be completely freeze-dried by the morning. How are you feeling?'

Tikaani grinned, stood up, and stretched. 'Never better!'

'Then get your boots on and we'll head up. Oh, and give me your water bottle. At least we can fill that up here . . .'

The ground slowly rose as they walked. Even back at the lake, high up the side of a mountain, there had been ups and downs and flat areas. Now there was no question. They were going *up*, and only up. Every step they took was fighting gravity, lifting them a bit higher. Their legs and thighs knew it and felt it. They still obeyed commands from the brain, but it was on the condition that they got all the body's reserve strength. There was nothing left for chat between the boys. They breathed deep of the thin air and they walked.

There were no more bare rocks, certainly no more plants to burn, nothing alive or dead to eat. Just a slope of smooth, unbroken snow. Beck led them up in long zigzags, grateful for the snowshoes on their feet. Without them the boys would have plunged into thigh-deep snow with every step and the climb would have been impossible.

But even that came to an end. Above them was a valley, with the ground rising up on either side. Between the slopes, where they would have to walk, the ground was jumbled and jagged in a hundred different shades of white and grey. In fact, Beck knew, it wasn't ground at all. It was a frozen river of ice pouring down the mountainside very, very slowly.

'It's going to get difficult now,' he said. 'This is a glacier.'

It had been marked on the map so he had been expecting it. At any rate, it meant they were still on course, still heading towards the pass through the mountains. But it was still a pain. The only way to reach the pass was straight up this valley – straight up the frozen river. After that they could carry on and be on dry land – or at least snowy land – again.

Tikaani craned his neck to follow the glacier's course.

'Do we go on it?' he asked.

'I'd rather not, but . . .'

Beck pulled the GPS out of his pocket, retrieved the batteries and reassembled the gadget. He squinted at the screen. According to the map, the mountain suddenly rose up almost vertically in a cliff – a curtain of rock a hundred metres high. Beck looked uphill and could see that for himself. The curtain rippled with frozen folds and creases. On the map, the pass came out in one of them. It was a clear area on the screen between two tightly clustered lines of contours.

'. . . but we've got to,' Beck sighed. He tilted his head back to look at the sheer peaks that were still over a thousand metres above them. Mighty geological forces had thrust these mountains out of the ground over millions of years. The same forces were very slowly pulling the mountains apart under their own weight. There were cracks in the sheer wall of rock – and that was what would help them. One of those cracks was the pass they were heading for.

'I don't see it,' said Tikaani, following his line of sight and mirroring Beck's thoughts.

'It'll be there.' Beck pointed with his hand, slicing

through the air straight ahead of them. 'Thataway. Look.' He held up the screen. 'See how close the contours are?'

Tikaani glanced at the glowing image. 'Uh-huh?'

'The closer they are together, the steeper it is in real life.'

'So . . .'

'So our pass will be a very narrow path between two very steep bits of rock. Don't sweat – we'll find it but we may have to be close to see it.'

The power display on the screen was almost flat, so Beck quickly switched it off again. He could navigate by eye for the time being.

'And from now on' – he shucked off his rucksack and opened it – 'we tie ourselves together.'

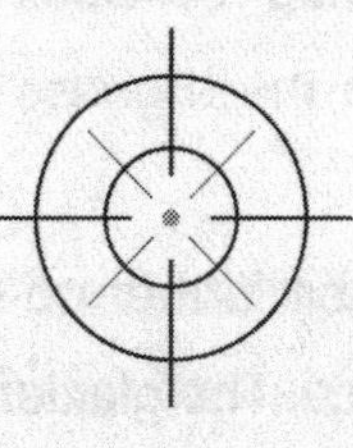

CHAPTER 24

They each had a length of home-made rope in their rucksacks. Beck tied the two ends together and tugged hard. The knot held.

'In case I run away?' Tikaani asked.

'The good news,' Beck explained, 'is this ice won't break beneath you like the lake did. The bad news – there'll be cracks in it. It weighs thousands of tons and there are huge stresses on it, so it develops crevasses, like I told you earlier. They may be covered up, so you have to look out for snow that dips a little and looks a bit darker. You fall into one of them, and it's a deep one, you ain't ever getting out.'

'So if you fall,' Tikaani said, fingering the rope thoughtfully, 'it's up to me to catch you and pull you up?'

'Yeah, if you could . . .' Beck made it sound like some small favour. 'And I guess I'll do the same for you.'

They walked a bit further up on firm land before stepping onto the ice. The glacier curved at the point where they were approaching it, and Beck knew that the outside bend is often where crevasses are found. It is the area where the strains on the ice are at a maximum.

'Stay a few metres behind me,' Beck instructed. 'Don't let the rope drag on the ground. Walk in my footprints, and every step you take' – he jabbed, hard, at the ice in front of him with his stick – 'test it first.'

'Even if you've just walked on it?' Tikaani asked.

'Even if. For all you know, I've just weakened it so it'll collapse under you!'

'Well, sure.' Tikaani shrugged. 'What else are friends for?'

They moved onto the ice, slowly at first, then with increasing confidence. Fortunately it was still covered with a layer of powdered snow that crunched and compressed beneath their feet. Later in the year, when all the snow had gone, they would have been walking on bare ice, slithering and sliding everywhere.

Beck headed for the middle of the glacier before turning uphill again. Crevasses were also common at a glacier's edge, where it dragged against the hard rock of the mountain. The middle should be flowing more smoothly.

They came to their first crevasse about twenty minutes later, a few hundred metres further up. After all their precautions, it wasn't hidden and it didn't swallow either of them up without warning. But it was still dangerous. It stretched right across the valley, from edge to edge. A gaping crack in the ice, about thirty metres deep and three across. Sometimes there was a thin span of ice across it; mostly it was just open to the sky. Beck guessed that the valley floor pushed up beneath the glacier at this point. It had put a stress on the ice that made it open up here.

'You know,' Tikaani said thoughtfully, 'I bet I could jump that. We throw our rucksacks over first, then we remove our snowshoes and take a run-up . . .'

Beck shook his head. 'You don't know how solid

the edges are. The far side might just crumble beneath you. We need an ice bridge.'

Tikaani looked at him. 'And I bet you know an ancient Anak method for making one of them?'

Beck smiled and shook his head again. 'Nature makes 'em; we just use 'em. This way.'

They walked slowly along the edge of the crevasse to the nearest of the bridges. It was about three metres long, from one side of the crevasse to the other, and about a metre wide. It sagged in the middle, which didn't fill Beck with confidence. He poked it with his stick. Immediately it split and tumbled into the crack.

'Not that one,' he said as the fragments hit the bottom and shattered into a million pieces.

They tried several more of the bridges. Not all of them crumbled, but . . .

Some of them were too narrow. Some Beck just didn't like the look of. He wanted good thick ice – several centimetres of it at least – that didn't sag. He wanted it to form an arch with the ends thicker than the middle. That way it would give itself extra strength.

None of them were exactly perfect. But time was

ticking away – time to save Uncle Al and, more immediately, to get over the mountains.

'After you,' said Tikaani politely, not taking his eyes off the thin bridge that was the best contender. It was thicker than the rest and it didn't shift when Beck poked it.

'Yup,' Beck agreed.

Tikaani peered into the depths. 'If you fall, I'm really not sure I can hold you . . .'

'Nor am I,' Beck agreed again, to Tikaani's obvious surprise. 'So take your pack off . . .'

The layer of snow on top of the glacier was a couple of feet deep. The boys scooped out a hole and buried Tikaani's rucksack. They then tied the rope to it. Now the rope stuck out of a pile of churned-up snow. The end was wrapped round Beck's waist.

'It'll never hold,' Tikaani said sceptically a few minutes later. 'It'll *never* hold!'

'You reckon?' he said with a grin. He hadn't believed it himself when he'd first seen this done. He passed the rope to Tikaani. 'Back off a couple of metres and give it a tug. Go on.'

Frowning with doubt, Tikaani took the rope and pulled. And pulled again. The buried rucksack stayed exactly where it was. He looked up at Beck, baffled.

'Snow's like that,' Beck told him. 'It's loose, it's fragile, it crumbles easily – but if you apply force to it, it can jam solid. You could pull the sack straight up, but you can't drag it through the snow.'

Tikaani looked from the buried pack, to the rope, to the crevasse. 'I still . . . can't *completely* believe it,' he admitted.

'And that's why I'm going first!'

Beck took off his snowshoes and moved out onto the bridge on all fours, with the rope round his waist, while Tikaani paid it out through his fingers behind him. If Beck had been standing, then all his weight would have been concentrated on his feet. On all fours, his weight was distributed.

The first time he put his hand down on the bridge, there was a very slight pause and then something gave way beneath him and his hand moved another couple of centimetres. Beck froze, convinced the bridge was about to collapse. Then he realized it was just like when he walked on the snow. The topmost layer was frozen and it put up the tiniest resistance before his weight broke through to the softer snow beneath. He forced out a very brief laugh and kept crawling, trying not to think of all the thin air the other side of this very thin bridge . . .

It was over very quickly – he only had to crawl a few metres, after all. All that fuss for such a short distance seemed silly until you remembered the alternative – dying in a frozen mass of broken bones at the bottom of the crevasse. He stood up and dusted himself down, then turned back to Tikaani with a big smile on his face.

'Your turn!'

Tikaani took off his snowshoes and dug up his rucksack on one side of the crevasse while Beck tied the rope around his own on the other and buried that. Tikaani tied his end of the rope around his waist, then dusted the snow off his pack, slipped his arms through the straps so that it was settled securely on his back, and crawled out over the bridge with much more confidence than Beck had done.

'*Whoa!*' Tikaani stopped almost at once, poised just past the edge of the crevasse. 'I felt something go.'

'Just keep going steadily,' Beck called.

Tikaani looked up at him anxiously. 'That's just—'

Suddenly the bridge crumbled and Tikaani vanished from sight.

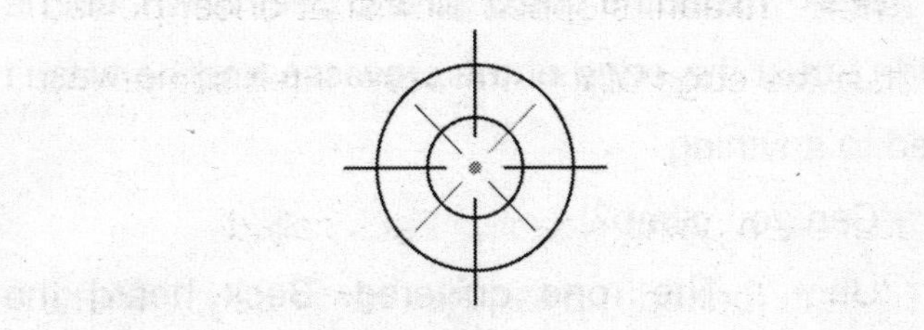

CHAPTER 25

'Tikaani!' Beck shouted. There had been a brief yell of surprise from his friend, but it had been cut short by an ominous thump. The rope and the buried rucksack held his weight, though the rope was taut and cut into the snow at the crevasse's edge. Tikaani was out of sight, dangling below on the end of the rope.

'Tikaani!' Beck called again. 'You OK?'

There was a pause.

'Yes.' Tikaani's voice came up out of the crevasse. He sounded winded. He would have thumped against the side as he fell. Beck pictured his friend dangling there. Neither boy was wearing any special kind of harness. The rope had been tied around their waists, so the loop would slowly squeeze Tikaani, cutting off his breath.

Beck wished he could go and peer down, but he didn't trust the edge of the crevasse and he wasn't tied to anything.

'Can you climb?'

'Uh . . .' The rope quivered. Beck heard the sound of Tikaani's boots scrabbling against the ice. Then the rope jerked as if a weight had yanked on it and he heard Tikaani swear.

'No. My boots just slip off the ice.'

To climb a wall of ice you needed proper equipment. Crampons. Axes. Sharp metal that would stick in. Beck looked around him for anything that would help. Anything. All they had was more rope . . .

Yes, he thought, the rope, of course. One end was tied to Tikaani. Only the middle bit was tied around the buried rucksack. The other end was still loose, coiled on the snow next to the pack.

'Tikaani? I'm sending some more rope down. Look out.'

Beck threw the free end of rope towards the crevasse. It uncoiled as it flew through the air and the end vanished into the crack in the ice. A moment later:

'Uh – got it. Now what?'

'Take hold of it with both hands. Pull it tight.'

The rope stiffened as Tikaani's weight pulled down on it.

'Now, brace your legs against the side of the ice and . . .'

'Yeah. Thanks. I think I've got it.'

Both ends of rope were completely taut now – the one that was tied to Tikaani and the one he was pulling on. They lay side by side on the ice, vanishing over the edge.

The length that was tied to Tikaani suddenly went loose. That meant Tikaani was climbing – his weight was no longer pulling on it. Beck allowed himself a grimly pleased smile and sat down in the snow, with his heels digging in. He took hold of the loose length and looped it around his body, then pulled gently until it was tight once more. Now Beck himself was a bollard, something to take the weight if Tikaani fell again. His friend would drop back into the crevasse, but not as far.

He heard scratchings and scrapings as Tikaani slowly clambered up. Then the rope jerked in Beck's hands as the other boy's full weight tugged on it again. Tikaani's weight yanked hard at him and he slid forward in the snow a few centimetres, braced against the force. But then his heels dug in and he stopped moving.

Again there was the thump of Tikaani's body hitting the side of the crevasse, and some furious Anak words he hadn't heard before.

'OK,' Beck called. 'So you slipped, but you're a bit higher.' And because Beck had gathered the rope in as Tikaani climbed, Tikaani was going to stay a bit higher. 'Just keep going . . .'

Bit by bit, Tikaani made his way up. He would hold onto the free end of rope and walk a metre up the ice. The rope tied around him would go loose and Beck would pull it in. When Tikaani's snowshoes inevitably slipped and he fell against the ice, he stayed at his new height.

After about ten minutes, Tikaani's head emerged above the lip of the crevasse. His face was contorted with effort, but he managed to bare his teeth at Beck in a grin of triumph. Beck kept up the tension on the rope while his friend slowly crawled over the edge. He only let go when Tikaani was well and truly safe.

Tikaani pushed himself up onto his knees. 'Please,' he croaked, 'just get us off this bloody ice.'

Beck laughed with relief. 'Certainly. If sir would like to step this way . . . ?'

It wasn't far – just another hundred metres until the glacier bent to the north, and they kept straight on. Even so they stayed roped together.

'It doesn't matter if there's only a metre or so to go,' Beck pointed out as they neared the edge. 'On a glacier like this you can't be too careful.'

But finally they were off the glacier and back on the mountainside. They could untie themselves and coil the rope back into a rucksack. They looked at each other and breathed out in relief.

'And we're almost there,' Beck told Tikaani. He glanced up ahead. The wall of rock was still a few hundred metres higher than they were, but it was only about half a mile distant. He pulled out the GPS again. 'It's . . .'

The glow of the screen faded away like a dying breath.

'Oh no!' Beck protested. 'No, no!'

He thumped the little gadget in his hand and the screen flickered briefly back to life. The power display was almost completely flat. He tried to fix the image in his mind before the GPS died for good. Beck was left staring at a small square of dead plastic. It was the best that advanced twenty-first-century technology had to offer, and was now as much use as a dead fish.

Or maybe not even that much use – at least they could have eaten a dead fish.

'Hey, no problem,' said Tikaani, straight-faced. 'I'm sure I saw a recharge socket back there. I think it was in the wall of the crevasse.'

Beck smiled ruefully. 'OK, it got us this far. And we still have the map.' He slipped the GPS into his pocket and turned his back to Tikaani. 'Could you get it out?'

Tikaani pulled the map from Beck's rucksack and they unfolded it together. The map was covered with symbols – contours, of course, and different hieroglyphs for rocks and trees and ice. It took a moment for Beck to assimilate it all and identify their position.

He wondered if maybe he hadn't been a bit too reliant on the GPS.

But the river that they had forded was easy to find – a wiggly blue line, deceptively thin. He remembered where the pass was too – the winding thread through the knot of contour lines. Their position had to be somewhere between the two. They had headed pretty well due west from the river. He trailed his finger along the map. Once he had found the cluster of dark lines that represented the glacier, he knew exactly where they were.

'So, we're here . . .' He looked up at the mountaintops. 'And the pass is here.' They would find it. He squared his shoulders. 'Ready for the last bit?'

'And then it's downhill all the way?'

Beck checked the map again. The pass itself crested a rise through the mountains.

'Once we're halfway through – you bet!'

'Oh boy, oh boy!' Tikaani said with feeling. 'Lead on!'

Up ahead, two rocky promontories protruded from the base of the cliff. They came down the slope in different directions, one to the south and one to the north. The boys were heading for the cliff in between. They kept their zigzag course up the slope but their destination was always in sight. The rocky arms stretched out like the mountain was welcoming them into its embrace. The cliff loomed up ahead of them. Beck scanned it quickly for the dark cleft that would indicate the opening of the pass.

'Not seeing it . . .' Tikaani murmured. He mirrored Beck's own thoughts. 'What exactly are we looking for?'

Beck remembered the pass on the map. On this side of the mountains it was tiny, its walls so close together that the threadlike contours on either side were a solid line. Beyond that it widened out into a much wider valley.

'This end – it won't be big. It might just look like a crack . . .'

A little further along the cliff, to their left, the mountainside bulged out slightly. Beck reckoned the pass would be just the other side.

'This way,' he said, and they changed course slightly. They came round the bulge . . .

. . . and faced nothing but sheer rock.

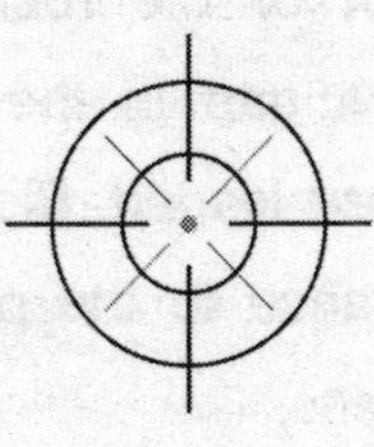

CHAPTER 26

The boys stared at it for a moment as if it might magically open up.

'Do we knock?' Tikaani asked after a moment.

Beck swore to himself. 'I'm sorry. I really thought this was it.'

'Hey, it must be around here somewhere,' Tikaani pointed out logically. Beck could hear the disappointment in his voice but his friend was quite right. 'We can go different ways to look for it.'

'Yes . . .' Beck really didn't want to split up, but it would save time. 'Don't go too far. A hundred metres, tops. We make sure we can see each other all the time, right?'

'Right.'

Tikaani headed south, Beck went north, carefully

scanning the foot of the rock face. Suddenly his eyes caught a gap in the cliff a couple of metres up. His heart leaped. Right! Of course! No one said the entrance to the pass had to be at ground level.

He kicked off his snowshoes and scrambled up the bare rock. The gap he was aiming for was no more than three metres wide, and it angled away from him. No wonder they hadn't seen it from a distance. He was careful to keep to his own rules, making sure Tikaani could see him, but at least he could get to the entrance. He stood there triumphantly and looked at . . .

. . . more rock. The gap went back for a few metres, and then its sides closed together. No pass.

Beck slowly turned away and climbed back down. He sat down and tied on his snowshoes.

Tikaani was trudging towards him. 'Nothing this way,' he reported. 'Not within a hundred metres anyway.'

'OK,' Beck sighed. 'We're going to have to go further. We'll look for it together.'

'Which way?' Tikaani asked.

Beck mentally tossed a coin. 'South,' he said, so they went back the way Tikaani had come.

They worked their way south along the cliff for five hundred metres, poking into every nook and cranny. Sometimes they climbed up the rocks as far as they could get to investigate more prospects like the one Beck had found. No luck. Finally they found themselves looking out over another crevasse in the snow. It had been carved out by a stream of melt-water that trickled by a few metres below. It was far too wide to cross and there was no way over it.

'If it's on the other side of that—' Tikaani began.

'It isn't,' Beck said shortly. Things like crevasses didn't show on the map – they came and went too quickly – but he was sure they were well past the likely area for the pass. The crevasse was nature's way of pointing this out and saying 'Turn round'. And so they did. They worked their way back again – Beck reckoned there was no harm in rechecking the cliff they had already covered – until they got to the point where they had started. Then they looked at each other, shrugged, and kept going.

'Hey . . .' Tikaani said at one point, and Beck's

heart leaped. Then he realized his friend was looking up at the crack he had already explored. He shook his head.

'Sorry. Done that.'

Tikaani's shoulders slumped and they trudged on. The cliff face bulged out ahead of them, and then curved back towards the mountain.

It took them a moment to realize it kept curving. Another minute and the cliff on their left was suddenly the left-hand side of a cleft going into the rock. They stood and looked at it for a moment. They'd had enough hope knocked out of them that they didn't get excited. Neither of them wanted to waste any more energy exploring another dead end.

'Is this . . . ?'

'Could be . . .'

'Well, someone else seems to think so,' Beck said, pointing at a line of tracks in the snow that also disappeared into the cleft.

They looked like a set of dog's paw prints. Each foot had four little toe marks arranged in a semicircle above a larger indentation. But both of them knew they didn't come from a dog.

The boys looked at each other.

'So what do we do if the wolf's still in there?' Tikaani asked.

Beck shrugged. 'Say, "Nice doggy"?' He craned his neck to peer further in. '"Woof"?'

The cleft was certainly deeper than the blind alley he had found earlier. You couldn't see all the way down it because it twisted and turned, but it went in the right direction. Yes, this could well be the pass . . . and it could be occupied. The paw prints didn't emerge again. The wolf was still in there. A hungry, possibly desperate predator. Beck didn't want to share a confined space with one of those.

Or, of course, he thought, it might have gone all the way through.

Well, there were two of them, and only one wolf, and they had sticks and they could probably scare it off. One thing was certain – they couldn't wait out here for ever.

'Come on,' Beck said, and they ventured in.

'This could be it,' Tikaani said after a minute. They walked in single file between high walls of rock on either side, still clutching their sticks against any possible wolf attack.

'Yup . . .' Beck agreed as the walls began to part. They could walk side by side now. There was a sharp corner up ahead. Sooner or later this pass would have to open out into a proper valley, and he thought that might be where it happened. 'Just round here . . .'

They turned the corner – and found their noses pressed against a sheer rock face. It was another dead end.

'*No!*' Tikaani shouted, a sharp bark of anger.

'Don't shout,' Beck said automatically. 'This is prime avalanche territory.' Though right then he wouldn't have minded if the mountain had dumped a thousand tonnes of snow right on top of them. He added: 'Sorry, mate. We just have to keep going.'

'And I'm hungry,' Tikaani muttered as they turned back. It had been a long time since they had eaten. Beck thought back and realized it had been well before they reached the glacier. They'd had enough on their minds since then to keep their thoughts off hunger. But now . . .

All their gathered food was gone. Beck had been

counting on getting through the pass and finding more food on the other side before hunger set in.

They could be in for a hungry night.

Tikaani paused and fingered the rock face. 'How about this?' he asked. Grey-green lichen sprouted out of the cracks in the rock. Tikaani pressed one of the spongy clusters with his finger. It shrank under the pressure, then sprang back again like rubber. 'I mean,' he added, 'you eat most stuff.'

'No good,' Beck told him with a shake of his head. 'It's too acidic for humans. If you wanted to eat it, you'd have to process it somehow to neutralize the acid.'

Tikaani pulled a face. 'And those rocks are starting to look mighty tasty too . . . So where did the wolf go?'

'Maybe he just dropped dead of hunger,' Beck muttered.

'Uh-oh . . .' Tikaani had found the paw prints again and was following them with his eyes. He crouched down. Then he crouched down a little further, his face almost pressed against the ground. 'Uh, Beck . . .'

Beck was by his side in a moment and they saw what had happened. There was another crack in the rock face here. Rather, there had been, once. There wasn't now because at some time – maybe a thousand years ago, maybe yesterday – a boulder had fallen down and blocked it off. The only way through was under the boulder – through that tiny, snow-clogged space that Tikaani had just discovered.

Or, he thought, you could go over the top.

'Wait here,' Beck said. He pulled off his snow-shoes and scrambled up the side of the rock. It was steep and he had to be careful, always making sure he had three secure anchors – feet or hands – before moving the fourth. But it wasn't that high, and in just a few moments he was standing on top of the boulder, gazing west. Then he called down to Tikaani.

'Come on up and admire the view!'

Tikaani joined him a minute later and they gazed out onto the pass.

Beck's guess had been right. The narrow cleft opened out into a wider path and, beyond that, a whole valley that continued up into the mountains.

'*Woo-hoo!*' Tikaani hooted with joy, and immediately bit his lip. 'Sorry,' he added, more quietly, crestfallen. 'I know, avalanches. But, woo-hoo, anyway.'

'Woo-hoo,' Beck agreed, grinning broadly. 'Get your snowshoes and let's go.'

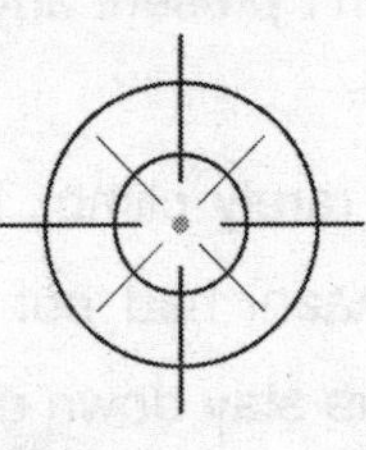

CHAPTER 27

'We Anak aren't known for our mountaineering skills,' Tikaani mused as they walked. 'I'm starting to see why . . .'

Beyond the narrow gully, the pass was wide. There was no sign of the wolf marks. Beck reckoned the wolf had passed this way a long time ago – long enough for snow to have buried the signs of its passing. The pawprints had survived on the other side of the boulder because it was sheltered there. Here the valley floor was thickly coated with snow, just like the mountainside behind them. It curved very smoothly in a deep U-bend from one side to the other; at the edges it turned sharply towards the sky, shedding the snow and revealing the sharp black rock beneath. Beck reckoned it would be easy to negotiate; it shouldn't present any major obstacles. On the other hand:

'That's why we rarely climb. There's absolutely nothing to eat.' Tikaani had put his finger on the problem. 'And so we stay down on the plains or by the sea.'

The valley was scoured by freezing, dry winds. Tikaani was right – there was little chance of finding anything to eat here.

'It makes sense,' Beck pointed out. 'You have to stay alive.'

'I know.' Tikaani sighed. 'I know. If you're going to live on the Arctic Circle, then survival comes first. You don't have time for luxuries like exploring or having fun. But you know' – he raised an eyebrow at Beck – 'nowadays, no one *makes* you live on the Arctic Circle.'

The pass still headed upwards. They hadn't quite reached the top yet, as Beck had pointed out earlier, but the ascent was much gentler than it had been before. Soon they were much higher than the cleft in the rock that had brought them here. Looking back, all they could see was sky, framed on either side by the valley walls. There may have been a bit of horizon in the very far distance. It was impossible to tell as it merged with the clouds gathering there.

The clouds . . . They were thick and swollen. Beck frowned. 'We need to press on,' he said. 'We really need to. We've lost a lot of time, and I don't want to be around when that lot gets here.'

Tikaani was looking ahead. 'That doesn't look like a rock . . .'

Something lay half buried in the snow. Rocks poking through were a common sight, but the lines of this were smoother and rounder. When they reached it, Beck was delighted to see what it was.

'It's a reindeer,' he said. He knelt down beside it and brushed the snow off the dead animal's abdomen with quick, rapid movements.

'Retirement was unkind to Rudolph,' said Tikaani.

The animal was the size of a small cow, covered in stubbly brown hair. Its eyes were clouded and blank. One of its antlers was broken and its neck was twisted round at an unnatural angle. Beck peered up the side of the valley to the rock ledges high above. The deer must have fallen from one of them, and rolled down the side of the valley when it hit the ground.

Beck unsheathed the Bowie knife and Tikaani's eyes went wide.

'You're kidding! We're going to eat this?'

'What, a nice venison roast?' Beck laughed. 'I wish. But there's no chance of a fire and cooking up here. No, we're not going to eat *this* . . . Not exactly . . .'

He sent up a quick prayer of thanks for the time he had spent with the Sami tribe. The most unappetizing thing they had taught him could be about to save their lives.

Beck pulled off his gloves and felt for the breastbone between the reindeer's front legs. Then he worked the knife's sharp point through the reindeer's skin and cut down towards its rear. Because the reindeer was frozen, cutting was hard work, but gradually the skin parted and the animal's abdomen opened up to the world. Now that the animal was dead, heart no longer pumping, there was little blood. Beck pulled back the layers of fat and tissue.

The reindeer's guts were like rubbery, bloated balloons packed expertly together. It couldn't have been dead for too long, Beck figured, because here, deep inside the animal, the innards weren't quite frozen and the smell of blood was sharp and metallic. It was both sweet and sour, rancid and pleasant. It wasn't designed to be let out into the air. It was supposed to be contained by the animal's body.

Tikaani watched with horrified fascination. 'OK. We're going to eat . . . what. Kidneys? Heart? I mean . . .' He started to gabble, maybe to hide his absorbed revulsion. 'OK, it's not exactly how you'd buy meat in the shops, but hey, I'm sure there're no germs up here and it probably doesn't matter that you didn't wash your hands first . . . '

'You're getting closer.'

'Oh God. Am I?'

Beck had reached the stomach. It was streaked with grey and green and splotches of dark red. Beneath his fingers it writhed and bulged like a balloon full of lumpy water. Beck probed it gently, then nodded, satisfied at what he had felt. He slipped his fingers into the cavity on either side and tugged. The stomach slithered out onto the ground like an alien slug that had been gestating in the corpse.

Beck stabbed it with the knife and a gurgling, semi-liquid mass poured out onto the snow. It smelled strongly of sick and Tikaani's face screwed up in disgust. Beck poked about in the mass with his fingers, then grinned and held up a couple of handfuls of stinking, sludgy lumps.

'This is what we're eating,' he announced.

'*You – are – kidding!*'

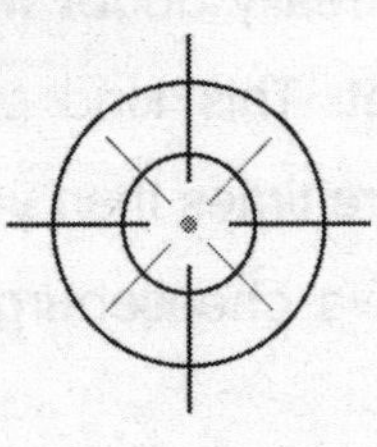

CHAPTER 28

By way of answer, Beck popped one of them into his mouth. 'Mm-mm! Reindeer moss.'

'Moss grows in reindeer?' Very reluctantly, Tikaani picked one of the lumps out of Beck's hand and held it up to study.

'No, that's just what it's called,' Beck said around his mouthful. He swallowed. 'It's really lichen. Remember I said the lichen on the rocks had to be processed? This is how it happens. Inside deer. They half digest it and then we can eat the rest.'

Tikaani still just looked at the lump in his hand. He prodded it with a finger. It squished and liquid oozed out when he squeezed it.

'Hey,' Beck said, more seriously. 'We really need to do this. We don't know when we're going to be eating again and I really doubt we'll get out of this pass before sunset. This kind of thing kept your ancestors alive more times than you'll ever know.'

'*They* didn't have cheeseburgers,' Tikaani said darkly.

'Neither do we, right now.'

'Right now . . . no,' Tikaani agreed. He held up the lump of moss. 'Oh God. I'm about to put it in my mouth. I am about to put a bit of reindeer poop in my mouth. I'm—'

'It won't have turned to poop yet. That happens further on.'

'Gee, thanks, that makes it so much better.' Tikaani closed his eyes and clamped his hand over his mouth so that the moss had to go in. Very slowly he started to chew, eyes still tight shut.

'Mrph,' he mumbled indistinctly. ''Kay. Tastes like . . .' He gulped a bit down. 'Y'know . . . I'm trying so hard *not* to think what it tastes like.'

'Like fresh green salad,' Beck suggested.

Tikaani's eyes opened, surprised and thoughtful. 'Well . . . yeah.' He swallowed again. 'Could do with some mayo but . . . yeah. Salad. Got any more?'

Beck smiled and passed him another piece.

They finished off the reindeer moss and washed it down with the last of their water. Then Beck showed Tikaani how to scoop fresh, powdered snow into their empty bottles.

'Now,' he said, 'tuck the bottle inside your clothes – though not right next to your skin – and your body heat warms it up. Give it half an hour and you've got a fresh supply of nice clean water again.'

'Can't we just eat the snow?' Tikaani asked as they heaved their rucksacks back on and set off once along the pass again.

Beck shook his head. 'Uh-uh. Snow isn't just frozen, it's way below freezing. It's like giving yourself frostbite in the mouth. Do it too much and you get sores, ulcers . . . so you don't do it. Besides, snow in your stomach will reduce your body temperature, and *that* means your body has to waste energy trying to warm itself up again. *Not* what we're trying to achieve.'

'Hmm . . .' Tikaani said thoughtfully; after that he was unusually quiet. Beck quite enjoyed walking silently. There were sharp, soaring peaks on either side. Ancient rock, millions of years old. A pure, unblemished snowfield. Crisp, fresh air unbreathed by any other set of lungs. All that the crowded, technological twenty-first century had to show for itself was two boys, dwarfed by the wilderness around them. The grandeur of nature was all the conversation Beck needed.

'I don't know much, do I?' Tikaani said suddenly.

Beck looked at him, surprised. 'Hey, you know enough!'

'Well, yeah, I know enough to cross the road, if I remember to press the "walk" button. I don't know enough to look after myself out here. *I'd* have eaten snow, except that I wouldn't – I'd have starved to death ages ago 'cos I wouldn't know which berries to eat. And eating stuff out of a reindeer's stomach? No way! But . . . I'm Anak. We knew all this once. It was second nature. But no one ever taught me . . .'

He fell silent again but Beck sensed he hadn't finished. A moment later, he added: 'Or maybe they tried and I just wasn't listening.'

Beck shrugged. 'You were listening. You knew

about bears and snowshoes and frostbite and . . . you know. You just need practice.'

'I suppose.' Tikaani laughed suddenly, his dark mood lifting. 'I wonder who was the first guy to eat reindeer moss? Who first looked at a dead deer and thought, *Mm-mm, never mind the meat, I bet what's in its stomach is really tasty*?'

Beck laughed with him. 'Maybe it was the same guy who was stuck in the middle of Africa and thought, *Dang, I've run out of wood, what can I burn for a fire? I know – elephant dung!*'

Tikaani hooted. 'Elephant . . . *dung*?'

'Yup. And it smells worse than you could possibly imagine.'

'No,' Tikaani said earnestly, 'it probably doesn't.'

The wind was picking up behind them. It was a freezing blast that would have been very unpleasant to walk into, but it was at their backs, blowing them on their way. Beck thought of the old Celtic blessing: 'May the road rise up to greet you, may the wind be always at your back.' This road was indeed rising up to greet them – they were still heading slightly uphill – and he reckoned that having the wind at your back was the nicest thing you could wish anyone.

'Could you get the map out, Tikaani?' he asked. He felt Tikaani tug at his rucksack and a moment later the map was passed to him. He unfolded it to show the pass and peered at it. He had to hold it quite close to see. If he was reading it right, then they should at least be out of the pass by sunset. There was still daylight left.

At least, there should be. He checked his watch. Yes, still some hours until sunset. But it was quite hard to even read the map in the gloom. As if something was blocking out the sun . . .

A reluctant instinct made him look across at the clouds. The fierce wind cut into his face and his heart sank. He knew immediately that they weren't going to get out of the pass that day. In fact, if he didn't do something right now, they weren't going to get out of the pass at all.

The storm had got here much faster than he had expected. It had been creeping up on them as they talked and laughed. The clouds were dark and swollen with a million tons of snow. The land below them was obliterated by snow and shadow. Standing on top of the mountain, Beck was at the same height as the storm. He wasn't looking up, he was looking straight at it. It was like staring into the eyes of a wild animal.

A wild animal that was charging at them, ready to wipe out anything in its path.

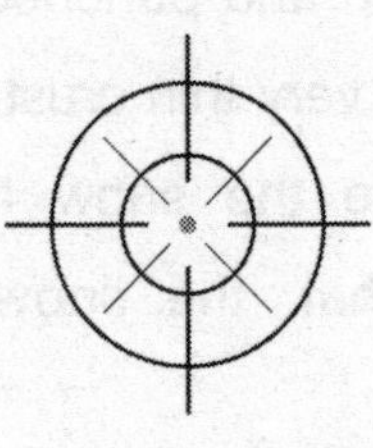

CHAPTER 29

Tikaani followed Beck's gaze. 'Oops. We're going to get snowed on?'

'If we're not careful we're going to get dead,' Beck said bluntly, 'Feel like some digging?'

But he was already trudging up the side of the valley as fast as his snowshoes would let him, before Tikaani could answer. He didn't go far – just until there was a good slope, about thirty degrees from horizontal. He thrust his stick into the snow and leaned all his weight on it. It went in as far as the very end, and even then it didn't hit anything. Excellent, Beck thought. There was probably a couple of metres of snow between them and the rock. That would do.

Tikaani had caught up. 'Digging?' he asked.

Beck knelt down and punched his fists into the snow. There was a very thin crust of ice on the top, called névé, where the snow had thawed then refrozen. Below that, the snow was fresh and powdery. Ideal.

'We're going to make a snow shelter,' he said. 'Start digging.'

Tikaani crouched down beside him and did as he was told, scrabbling away like a human terrier. Their mittened hands made excellent shovels. 'We just burrow down into the snow?'

'Exactly!' Beck agreed. He grinned without humour, and explained as their hole got deeper. 'Snow insulates. It keeps cold out and warmth in—'

'Excuse me,' Tikaani interrupted, though he kept digging. 'What kind of residence are Inuit famous for?'

'Huh?' Beck frowned for a moment, then his face cleared. 'Oh, yes. Right!'

Tikaani was thinking of igloos, which were built on exactly the same principle. Snow, packed solid, was a good construction material and an excellent insulator. Beck probably couldn't tell

Tikaani anything he didn't already know about snow.

'Have you ever been in a snow shelter?' he asked.

Tikaani shook his head. 'No. They're generally used by hunters and I've never been hunting. Or by people stuck out in storms . . .' He smiled at Beck. 'And I'd never done that either, until today. My dad was always very careful, making sure we didn't get caught in a whiteout.'

'Uh-huh.' Unlike Tikaani, Beck had experienced a whiteout – deliberately. With a rope around his waist, so that he could be dragged to safety, the Sami had sent him out into a snowstorm just to see what it was like. He hadn't been able to see a thing – not even which way was up or down. His sense of direction had vanished in about thirty seconds. Everywhere he looked, any way at all, there was just that whirling, ravenous white. If you got caught in a whiteout, the only answer was to stop moving and make a shelter. If you kept going, then you wouldn't just get lost. You might not be able to tell if something was ground or just air full of snow, so you could fall and not even realize until you hit bottom.

By now there was a sizeable pile of freshly dug snow around them. Beck scooped some up into a block and squeezed it together. The loose powder compressed into a solid mass with only a little pressure.

'So we've still got time to have a snowball fight?' Tikaani asked sceptically.

'Not really.' Beck plonked the block down next to the hole and scooped up some more. 'This hole is going to be our entrance, and so we need to block out the wind. This will be a little wall.'

Tikaani looked at the hole they were digging, realizing something for the first time. 'This is facing right into the wind. It's just going to fill up with snow again. Shouldn't we dig on another slope, away from the wind?'

Beck shook his head. 'The snow can just blow down a slope like that and bury everything there. If we're on the windward slope, we know the snow will always blow past us, keeping the entrance free. So we use this wall to keep the wind out of our hole. Keep digging – I'll give you a hand in a minute.'

It only took a couple of minutes for Beck to build

his wall. It didn't need to be high and it didn't need to be perfect. The blocks were crude and misshapen, but they stuck together. Even that reduced the wind speed significantly, and the boys felt the difference. It was as if warmth was a flower inside them, and suddenly it could put out a tiny little bud that hadn't been there a moment ago.

After about fifteen minutes the hole was deep enough for the two boys to crouch in, side by side. They were below the level of the snow and they could keep digging while the wind raged above them. It was already much stronger than it had been when the first snow was falling. It whipped past them – above them – in whirling clusters that stung the face whenever one of them peeked out. Inside the hole it was a couple of degrees warmer already.

'We spend the night like this?' Tikaani asked hopelessly.

Beck smiled. 'Hey, we've only just begun!'

He took a final look outside, ducking as a particularly strong burst of snow came swirling towards him. A shape moved within it – a white shadow that glided with the wind.

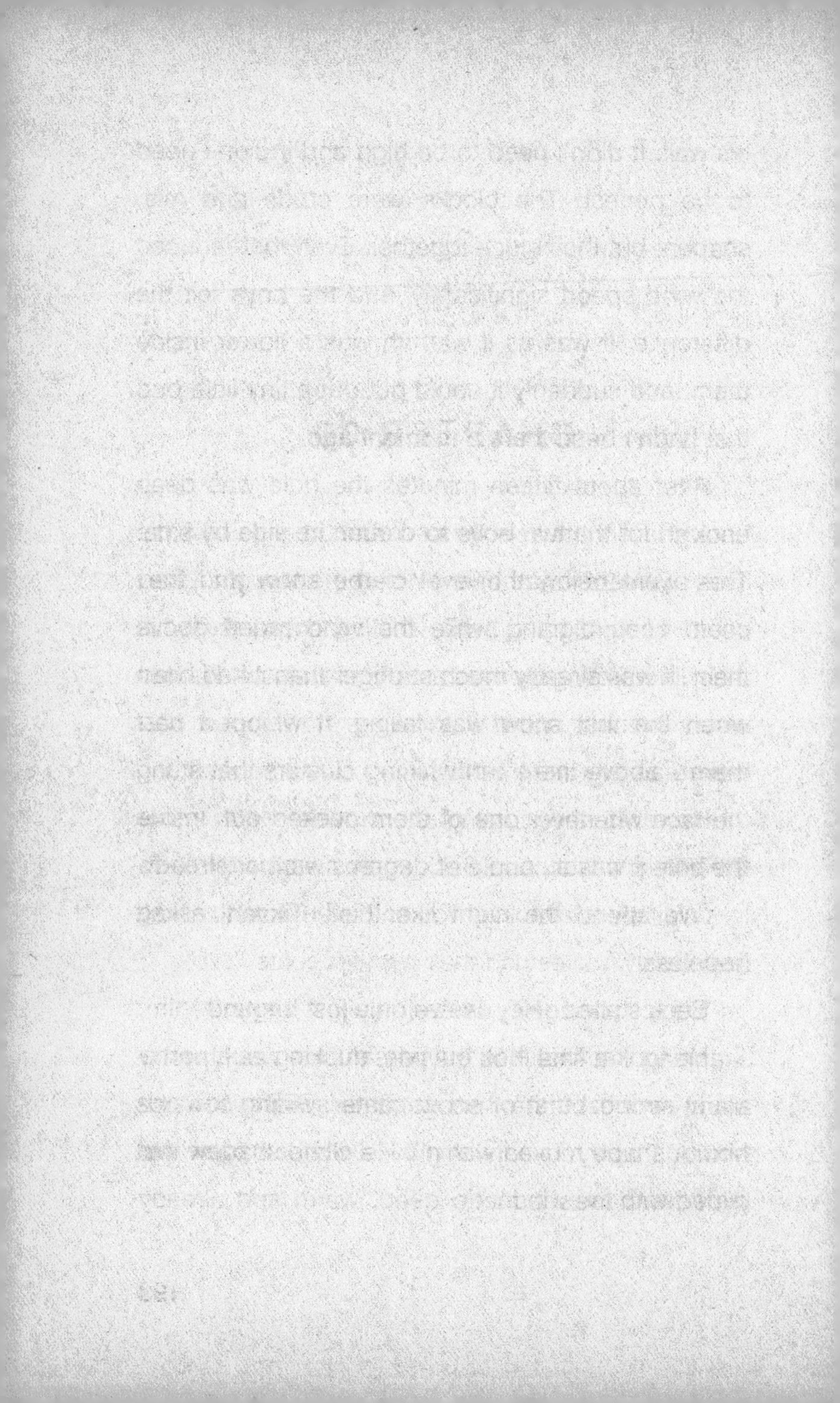

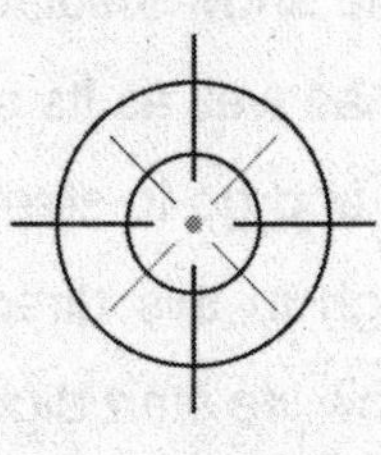

CHAPTER 30

Beck's every muscle tensed and he strained his eyes at where it had been. Where he *thought* it had been. It might have been whirling snowflakes, his brain interpreting them as a particular shape. He had barely thought about it for ages now, but it had looked awfully like a wolf.

However, the coming storm was much more lethal than a wolf, and Beck knew a wolf on its own was unlikely to attack. It wouldn't even want to share their cave. Wolves had their own fur coats.

'Deep enough?' Tikaani called behind him, snapping Beck back to the present. He would worry about wolves if he had to, later. Right now he wouldn't worry Tikaani at all. He climbed back into the hole. It was a metre deep, warm and already pleasantly quiet. The snow insulated them from the sound of the storm as well as its strength. It was so tempting to curl up and go to sleep . . . but not yet.

'It's deep enough in this direction,' he agreed, peering around. 'Now we start digging up again . . .'

And so their digging angled upwards, beneath the surface of the snow, careful not to break out into fresh air again. It took another hour to dig out the cave to Beck's liking, but the urgency was gone. Once they were safely inside, they could widen their excavation. When they finished they were covered in powdered snow, but that was easy to brush off and they could admire their handiwork.

The final chamber was almost three metres wide and one and a half high. The floor was a flat platform big enough for the two of them to sleep side by side. Because they had dug upwards beneath the snow, it was higher than the entrance. The wind was blocked out by Beck's snow wall and their rucksacks, which provided an extra barrier between them and the outside (and would also keep out any wolves that came visiting, Beck thought). The air was warm and still. The sound of the storm was a distant echo, there if they listened out for it. It could have been on the other side of some good double glazing.

'Cold air sinks,' Beck said, pointing back at the entrance. Even to his own ears his voice sounded muffled. The snow was absorbing vibrations. 'Up here we'll be good and warm. But help me smooth down the walls, or it'll drip on us.'

They worked together silently for a while. Tikaani blew out of his mouth a couple of times. It swirled in front of him. 'I can still see my breath,' he said.

'Good.' Beck smoothed down the final patch of snow and looked around. 'If it gets too warm, it'll collapse. But it'll be warm enough for us. It'll never drop below zero inside here, anyway. You'd better put your wet clothes out, by the way. They'll have frozen dry by the morning.'

'Compared to out there it's the tropics,' Tikaani agreed, with a nod back at the entrance. He opened up his rucksack for his wet things. 'Where do we put the jacuzzi?'

Beck chuckled as he laid out the tarpaulin where they were going to sleep. The floor was made of snow. They still needed insulation or the heat would be sucked out of their bodies. 'We'll do that tomorrow, right after we install the flat-screen TV and cable.'

'Hey, excellent! I can catch up on some good TV.'

Beck took all the loose items from their rucksacks and laid them inside the tarpaulin; spare clothes – even the rope – would keep them off the snow. Then he reached into his coat and pulled out his water bottle. He shook it and heard the contents slosh around. As promised, the snow had melted.

'And we have fresh water on demand,' he pointed out. 'Purer and cheaper than anything you could buy in a bottle back home.'

'Hey, yeah.' Tikaani took a long swig from his own bottle. 'Maybe we should have dug a bathroom too. This lot will come out eventually.'

'We have a bathroom.' Beck pointed down at the entrance.

Tikaani looked unenthusiastic. 'Yeah, I was hoping to avoid going outside again . . .'

Beck shook his head. 'Not outside. It's not worth losing the warmth. Just go down there. Let the snow absorb it.' He looked at where Tikaani's clothes were spread out. 'Just try not to go on those.'

It was nearly dark outside now, and even darker in, with no torch or fire. And they were both tired. They lay down on the tarpaulin and Beck heard Tikaani stretch luxuriously.

'I don't care that we're in a hole in some snow on the top of a mountain. This is better than any hotel.'

Beck smiled to himself in the darkness. It wasn't how he had intended to end the second day of their journey, but it was better than it might have been.

'They taught you this when you were in Finland?' Tikaani asked.

'This? No. This comes from a weekend in the Cairngorms.'

'Where are they?'

'Scotland. Closer to home.'

'Oh.' Then: 'My ancestors really did know their stuff, didn't they?' Tikaani sounded more thoughtful, going back to their conversation earlier.

'You know it too,' Beck answered. 'It just takes a while to come back.'

'Yeah.' Tikaani yawned. 'Bit by bit,' he mumbled . . .

And soon after that, it was obvious from his regular breathing that he was fast asleep. Beck lay and listened to the storm for a bit longer. He didn't invite sleep because he knew it would come naturally.

Like the previous night, he thought of Al. He hadn't thought so much of his uncle during the day – there had been enough on his mind to keep him occupied. How was Al doing? Had the storm hit him too? His little shelter should be OK. He would be in serious trouble if the fire went out, though. Beck just had to trust that Al knew enough to look after himself.

In his last waking moments, he sent up a silent prayer that the storm wouldn't last long. They didn't have enough food or water to survive a long imprisonment.

They could be warm, and dry, and sheltered, and still starve. Their warm cave could just as easily become an icy tomb.

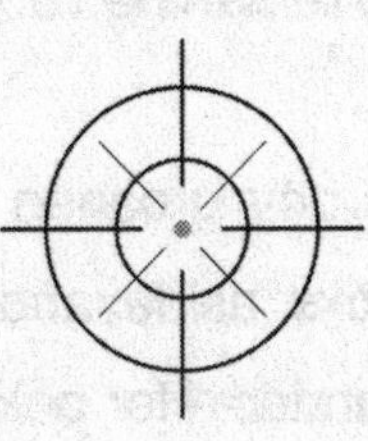

CHAPTER 31

Beck was woken by a sharp stab of hunger in his guts. He winced and rolled onto his side. He was pretty certain he must have slept. He had a sense that time had passed without his knowledge.

Something had changed and it took a while to work out what. There was more light, for a start. A white glow further down the tunnel forced its way past the rucksacks in the entrance and outlined them with silver. And it was quiet. Even allowing for the muffling effect of the snow, it was quiet. No wind blowing.

Light plus quiet equalled no storm. No storm equalled no reason to hang around a moment longer.

He gave Tikaani a hard nudge. 'Wakey,

wakey! We have to leave the room for the maid to clean.'

While the other boy groaned and stirred, Beck kicked the rucksacks aside and worked his way back down the tunnel. He poked his head out of the mountainside like an animal emerging from hibernation.

It was the third day of their journey – and, Beck fervently hoped, the last. He wanted to be off these mountains and down in Anakat by sunset. The signs were good. The sky was blue and the sides of the valley were pristine white. The snow wall had held up against the wind. All the jumbled, torn-up snow left over from their digging was smoothed and rounded by a fresh coating.

Tikaani poked his head up beside him and blinked sleepily. 'I am so hungry. Is there any food?'

'Plenty,' Beck assured him. He threw his rucksack out onto the snow and scrambled out after it. 'As much as you could ever want.' He pulled out his water bottle and started to pack it with snow.

Tikaani looked around at the stark crags above

and smooth, unblemished snow all around. 'Where?' he asked suspiciously.

Beck pointed westwards, down the valley. 'A couple of hours' walk in that direction.'

Tikaani groaned.

In fact it took more than a couple of hours, but it felt like less. In no time at all, they both realized the valley was angling downhill. They were over the top of the mountains. That alone gave them a huge psychological boost. Charged with energy, they plunged down through the snow.

Before long they were out of the pass and onto the mountainside again, two specks on an infinite sheet of white. It seemed like all of Alaska was laid out before them, covered with a fresh coat of snow from the night's storm. Far below were meadows and the tops of trees. Sometimes a sparkle caught the eye as sunlight shone off fresh water. Towards the horizon, sky and land came together, sealed with a strip of glittering blue sea.

'Anakat's down there,' Beck said.

Tikaani's grin split his face from ear to ear. 'Oh, yeah!'

The way down grew steeper. Beck remembered the magic figure – two degrees for every hundred metres. And this time it was getting warmer. At first they went down the same way as they had walked up on the other side, zigzagging from side to side. But, Beck reckoned, it would be so much easier – not to mention shorter – if they went straight down . . .

'OK,' he said. He pulled off his snowshoes and hung them on his rucksack while Tikaani looked on. 'There's an art to this. You take large strides . . .'

He set off downhill for a few paces, deliberately lengthening his stride. Each time his foot came down he put his weight on his heel and kept his leg straight. His weight drove his boot into the snow and he went in to above his knees. But with each step the snow compressed beneath him and provided him with an automatic foothold.

'Try it,' he called back up to Tikaani. 'We'll take a few practice steps to start with.'

Tikaani took one step and paused. His position was comical, one leg buried almost to the thigh in snow, the other at an awkward angle and a little further uphill. 'OK, that worked . . .'

He brought the other leg down. 'Yeah, I can do this . . .'

And again, and again. He lurched past Beck. 'This is easy!'

Beck set off quickly after his friend.

It *was* easy. The practice steps turned straight into the real thing. The rhythm of their strides took their bodies and their momentum did the rest. They plunged through the snow like a pair of ploughs, sending up sprays of powder with each stride. Beck tried to keep up with Tikaani but his friend was actually drawing ahead. From the way Tikaani was leaning forward, his arms waving, Beck wondered if the other boy was getting out of control. Sure enough, a moment later Tikaani tipped forward and cartwheeled down the slope ahead of him.

'Tikaani!'

Tikaani kept rolling until he smashed into a snowdrift in an explosion of snow. Beck hurried down after him. Tikaani was just lying there, covered in snow, his body quivering slightly. Beck wondered if he was in some kind of shock. But as he approached, he realized Tikaani was shaking with laughter.

'That was fun! Let's do it again!'

Their way down the mountain after that was much faster than their way up. Before long there wasn't enough snow to support that method of travelling. Then came the moment when Beck stumbled on something. He kicked the snow aside and saw rock. They were almost off the snow altogether.

Patches of dry earth began to show. Soon it was hard to tell if they were on snow with bare patches of ground, or ground with occasional snowy areas. Tough, scrubby grass appeared underfoot.

They came to a stream, running with clear, fresh meltwater. On the way up, streams had been irritations – they were just obstacles to overcome. This one was a welcome companion, flowing down towards the same warm, low land they were heading for. They could drink liquid water straight from the source again without having to wait for it to melt.

They followed it into the trees. Trees! The woods seemed thicker this side of the mountains. Less bare tundra, more wood, stretching all the way to the distant band of the sea.

'OK,' Beck said. 'I promised you breakfast.' It didn't take long to find a fallen trunk. He pried off a section of bark with the Bowie knife and a small colony of wriggling grubs tried to squirm away from the daylight.

Tikaani looked at them without enthusiasm. 'I know I ate something out of a dead animal's stomach yesterday,' he said, 'but even so . . .'

Beck picked up a large grub the size of his finger and held it for inspection. It writhed and coiled like an animated piece of string. He thought for a moment. 'Every time I eat one of these, it's like it takes a poop on my tongue in revenge.'

'*Every* time? You mean, you've done it more than once and you still haven't learned?'

Beck grinned and bit the head off the grub, then spat it out and swallowed the body. 'You know these things are eighty per cent protein? Even beef's only twenty per cent.'

'Yummy.' Tikaani picked up a couple, studied them philosophically and crammed them into his mouth. He pulled a face. 'You got fries to go?'

'They taste better if you bite the heads off . . .'

'Now he tells me!'

Beck suddenly held up a hand. 'Listen,' he said. 'Hear that?'

Tikaani strained his ears. 'Only water,' he said. It came from lower down, through the trees – the sound of a torrent, rushing and gurgling over rocks.

Beck beamed. 'Exactly! Still hungry?'

'What, after that delicious feast? You bet.'

'Well then, let's see if we can get something even better!'

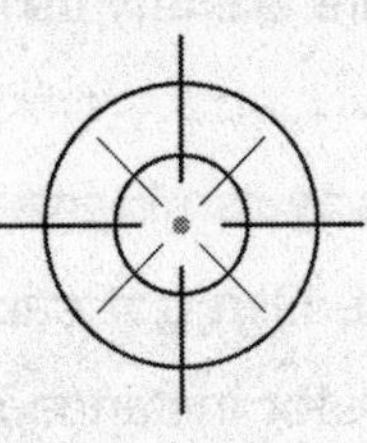

CHAPTER 32

The river came down from the mountains in joyous leaps and bounds, tumbling from ledge to ledge and pool to pool. When the boys came across it, it was flowing purposefully over a wide bed of gravel. Stones and rocks rippled beneath the sparkling water. It was shallower than the river they had forded two days earlier, and – thankfully – calmer. The water's flow was a quiet hurry, rather than the deadly rush that had presented them with such difficulties.

'Fish,' Beck said.

'Rod and hook?' Tikaani asked sceptically.

Beck smiled. 'Who needs 'em? Look.' He pointed over at the bank where the river flowed around a number of small boulders. The spaces between the rocks made natural little pools. 'Let's check to see if there are any fish caught over there. I'll look over here.'

There weren't any fish in the pools, which didn't really surprise him. Fish got caught in pools when the river level fell – for instance in the heat of summer. At this time of year the river would be rising constantly, swollen by the meltwater.

'Right. For my next trick, ladies and gentlemen, I will require a couple of water bottles.' Beck delved into his rucksack and dug out two of their spares. They had once held lemonade, but he had poured that out back at the plane (it seemed almost a lifetime ago). The bottles were cylindrical and plastic and transparent, perfect for his needs.

He looked up at Tikaani. 'Could you see if you can dig out some grubs or worms or something?' he asked. 'Bring 'em over here.'

Three days ago, Tikaani would have rewarded him with a blank look or an expression of disgust. Now he just shrugged. 'Sure.'

Beck used the knife to cut each bottle in half across its width, and sliced off the tip where the cap twisted on. It made the spout just big enough for a fish to get through. Tikaani used a pointed rock to dig into the soil of the river bank and came back a moment later with a couple of writhing worms.

'Perfect!'

Beck dropped them into the bottom halves of each bottle and forced the top halves in after them, upside down. Now each bottle was something like a double layered cup, with the worms squirming around in the gap between the two halves.

'There's nothing fish like more than a bit of worm,' he told Tikaani. 'Now we just need to decide where it's going . . . And that is over here.'

They went back to the rocks they had just been checking, which were on the outside bend of a wide curve in the river.

'Fish get carried round the bend on the outside,' Beck explained. He leaped onto the nearest rock from the bank and carefully studied the channels where the water flowed. Yes, he decided, this would do. He knelt down and plunged the first bottle trap into the water, with the open end facing into the current.

Freezing water splashed against his hand but he

made sure the trap was wedged into position before letting go.

Then he did the same with the second bottle trap on the other side of the rock. The water stripped the warmth from his arm and cold seemed to gnaw at his bones. He was just grateful that he didn't have to put more than his hand in.

'And now we wait . . .' he said. 'Stay there and stay still. They can't see us clearly but they can tell when something moves . . .'

Shapes moved under the water in the pool, graceful and sinuous. They flickered over the gravel bed from shadow to shadow. Beck remained perfectly motionless.

'Lovely, lovely worm . . .' He tried to project his thoughts telepathically at the fish. 'Yum yum yum . . .'

'How long does it take?' Tikaani asked.

'Depends on how hungry they are.'

'They can't be as hungry as I am . . .'

Beck smiled. 'If they won't take the bait then we can try and drive them in. Get in the water upstream and wade down here. They'll hear us coming and try to get out of the way.'

'You mean, get wet again?'

'Exactly, which is why I don't want to do it. Or I can try tickling them.'

'*Huh?*' Tikaani looked baffled.

Beck grinned. Mindful of the fish in the water, he still didn't move. 'You lie on the bank with your hand in the water. You do it very, very slowly so the fish doesn't notice you're not just a branch or a piece of weed. You slowly move your hand under the fish . . .'

'That's not tickling, that's assault!'

Beck chuckled, though he never took his eyes off the water.

'. . . and then you flip it out onto the bank. And you make sure it *does* go on the bank. First time I tried it, I just managed to flip the fish further into the middle of the river.'

'Then it told all its friends not to go anywhere near the hungry human on the bank?'

'Exactly . . .'

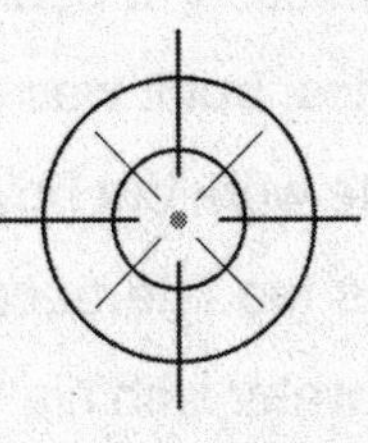

CHAPTER 33

Beck craned forward slowly, not wanting to disturb anything. A fish was nosing at one of the traps. The problem with this method of fishing was you didn't get to choose what kind of fish you caught. In this case they had struck lucky – it looked like a trout. About fifteen centimetres long, brown and speckled, one big fin on its back and several smaller ones along its stomach.

The trout was cautious, but then it obviously remembered it was hungry and swam in. The funnel shape of the top half of the bottle guided it towards the worm that was trapped between the two halves. It wriggled through the gap and pounced on the worm, gulping it down in a couple of swallows. Now it was between the two halves of the bottle and its tiny fishy brain was confused. It could see light through the transparent sides, but it was in a confined space and it couldn't quite work out how to get out again.

And then it was too late because Beck whisked the trap out of the water with his hand over the open end. He held it up triumphantly.

'We have fish!' He handed it to Tikaani, who took it gingerly. The trout was wriggling enough to splash water out of the trap. 'Take it to the bank, hold it upright and *don't* let it go.'

Tikaani had the sense to retreat a safe distance from the river. Even if he did drop the trap, the trout wouldn't end up back in the water.

Now Beck just had to wait for a fish to swim into the second trap. It took a bit longer but eventually another fish fell for it. He wasn't sure what kind this one was, but that didn't matter. It was food.

He sauntered with the second trap back to where Tikaani was waiting. His friend was almost quivering with eagerness.

'What is it? What kind of fish?'

Beck shrugged. 'No idea.'

Tikaani looked blankly at him. 'Supposing it's

poisonous?' He was actually hopping about, ready to get his fish out and stuff it in his mouth. But his natural caution came first.

'It won't be – freshwater fish are edible.'

'I feel like I could eat this whole!' Tikaani said. He managed to control himself a little longer. 'So how long now? You're going to make a fire, I suppose, and—'

'A fire?' Beck asked. 'What's that?'

He thrust his hand into the trap and grabbed his fish by the gills. While it was still wriggling in protest, he pulled it out and dropped the trap so he could hold it firmly with the other hand too. Then he bit firmly into it, halfway along the back, severing the spine. Juices spurted into his mouth. Fresh, moist, slippery meat slithered into his mouth.

He could feel the scales rubbing off on his face. He worked his way along the fish's back, tearing the tender meat off its fragile bones. Finally he lifted his face triumphantly to Tikaani.

His friend was staring at him with an expression of . . . horror? Fascination? Beck wasn't sure because Tikaani came to a decision with an almost visible effort. He grabbed hold of his own fish and did exactly what Beck had done.

'Just eat along the back,' Beck told him. 'And the sides, but be careful you don't bite into the guts. You really don't want to.'

Tikaani grunted indistinctly, his mouth full of raw fish. And that was all either of them said for the next couple of minutes as they finished off their meal.

'*Mm!*' Tikaani exclaimed. He dangled the chewed corpse in his hand. 'Sushi extreme. I had no idea I could be so hungry.'

'The problem' – Beck picked the last few scraps off his fish's backbone; it was a fiddly task, requiring concentration – 'with fire . . . is' – finally there was no more meat – 'it dries the fish out, soaks up all the juices. This way you get the full, natural goodness. Gives you strength, gives you moisture . . .'

'Keeps you alive,' Tikaani agreed. He looked hopefully at the traps. 'Any more?'

Beck laughed. 'Yeah, easy. 'Cos if there's one thing fish love more than a nice tasty worm, it's the guts of their friends.'

'Gee. I'd hate to be a fish's enemy . . .'

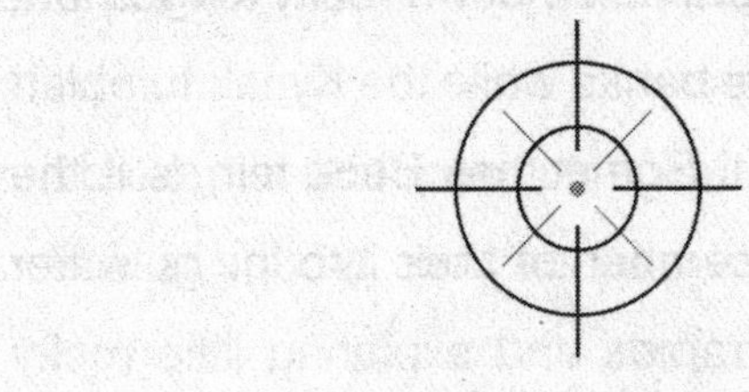

CHAPTER 34

The boys baited the traps with fish guts and caught two more. They ate them raw again with just as much enjoyment and energy. Then, with their hunger satisfied and a good drink inside them, they carried on along the river.

Beck had thought about whether to cross it, but decided it wasn't necessary. Unlike the last river, it wasn't in their way. According to the map, the river was called the Kynak. It continued to fall down from the mountains for a couple of miles, then curved sinuously across flat land. It went in roughly the direction they wanted to go and emerged into the sea very near Anakat. As a guide to navigation, it was pretty well infallible.

And so for the next couple of hours the boys

went with it. They scrambled down rocky ledges and walked along gravel banks while the Kynak tumbled along next to them. Sometimes Beck felt as if the river was a third member of their group, its water scampering down rapids and exploring little rocky pools like a small child.

'Hey, Beck.' Tikaani stopped suddenly and crouched down. Beneath a bush was a small, groundhugging plant with oval green leaves and red berries. They were perfect little spheres that looked almost like tomatoes, but smaller. 'Isn't this . . . ?'

Beck grinned. His friend was turning into quite the explorer. 'Yup, it's lingonberries and we can eat 'em. Good work, Tikaani.'

Tikaani was already tucking in. The spirits of both boys lifted yet further. They were back in a land that could feed them.

While Tikaani was searching around for more food, Beck studied the river. The last set of rapids had been a quarter of a mile earlier. Now it had flattened out and flowed smoothly.

He pulled the map out to check. Higher up, the river had come through a cluster of contour lines that meant a sharp change in height. Up there you couldn't walk along it for more than a hundred metres or so before hitting another set of rapids or a waterfall. But all that seemed to be behind them. As far as he could tell, the river should be level from here on. The ground would rise and fall but the river had cut its own little valley and the riverbank was littered with driftwood.

'Hey, Tikaani,' he called. 'How are your feet?'

Tikaani looked sideways at him. Then he wiggled his feet experimentally, one at a time. 'They're a bit sore. Still got five toes each, as far as I can tell. Why?'

'Oh,' Beck said innocently, 'I thought I could help them out a little . . .'

Tikaani just looked at him.

'We're going to make a raft,' Beck decreed. 'The river's going the same way we are so why not let it take the strain?'

'OK . . .' Maybe Tikaani was getting used to Beck's schemes. They were never quite what he expected but they seemed to work. 'How?'

A good question. Beck thought, briefly and

wistfully, of the raft he and his friends had built the previous year in Colombia. It had been a proper, industrial-strength, ocean-going raft that they had called the *Bella Señora*. It had been made of balsa and bamboo. They'd had all the resources of a forest and a household to call upon to make something solid and seaworthy. It had saved their lives, survived a shark attack and lasted several days at sea.

This raft wasn't going to be quite so impressive. But it would float, which was all he could really ask of it.

'OK.' He gave Tikaani instructions as to what to look for. 'We need two big pieces of wood – as straight as possible and at least this thick.' He held his hands about half a metre apart.

'It's going to take a long time cutting off one of those with your knife,' Tikaani said thoughtfully.

'We shouldn't need to.' Beck looked along the banks at all the driftwood. Rivers carried all kinds of natural junk along with them. The Kynak was swelling with meltwater – but later in the season the water would be much higher. When the water level had dropped the previous winter, anything drifting in the water would have been stranded on the banks. 'Let's collect as much of this driftwood as we can.'

It was easier said than done to find wood that matched his specifications. There was driftwood aplenty but it was mostly not thick enough, or long enough, or both. They had to widen the search by pressing into the woods, away from the river.

Beck was awkwardly aware of passing time. They weren't just doing this for fun, they were doing it to reach Anakat and save Uncle Al. Time spent building a raft now should save time later – but if he decided it was taking too long, they would just have to drop the idea and keep walking.

But they found the wood eventually. The two pieces were both about the right width but different lengths – one over two metres long, the other only about one and a half. They were heavy, and Tikaani and Beck had to carry the pieces between them back to the river bank.

'These are the main floats for the raft,' Beck

explained. They put the two branches down on the ground, parallel to each other, about a metre apart. They then laid smaller driftwood branches across them at right angles. 'These others are just for support, and to hold the deck.'

Then Beck delved into the very bottom of his rucksack and triumphantly produced more of the coiled wire he had salvaged from the plane. 'I just knew this would come in handy!'

He used the wire to lash the bits of wood together into a wooden frame, about a metre and a half long and a metre wide.

'And the deck?' Tikaani asked.

'You're carrying it. Get the tarp out of your rucksack . . .'

They stretched the tarpaulin out over the frame and used bits of rope to lash it to the wood. Finally they stepped back and admired their work. Beck looked at it critically; Tikaani beamed with pride as if they had just built the *Queen Mary*.

Well, Beck thought, it's not the *Bella Señora* but it will do.

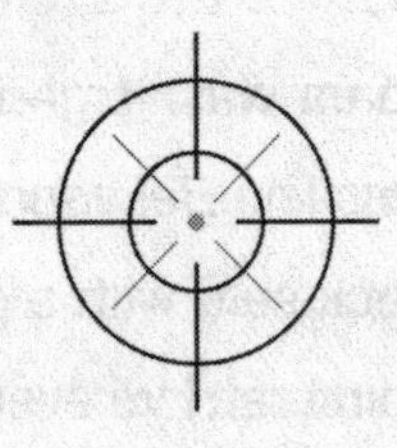

CHAPTER 35

Tikaani stood back to survey the raft. 'It needs a name,' he decided.

'You choose,' replied Beck.

'OK.' His friend thought. 'The . . . um . . . the . . . something Alaskan. The *Walrus*? The . . .'

'Keep thinking,' Beck told him, and turned back towards the trees. There was one more item they needed and he had seen just the thing earlier on. It was a long branch, thin but sturdy, that he could use as a steering pole. The raft didn't have a sail or a rudder. The current would carry it in the right direction, but they had to steer it somehow. They would have to pole along the bottom.

'The *Orca*?' Tikaani suggested when he got back with the length of wood. 'The *Polar Bear*?'

'The *Igloo*?'

'Ha ha . . .' Tikaani wasn't giving up. 'We could combine our names. The *Bekaani*.'

'Or the *Tick*,' Beck said with a grin.

'Hey, this is the first raft I've ever made and it gets a name!'

'Well, give me a hand meanwhile . . .'

The raft was too heavy to lift so they had to push it into the water. Beck had set the floats at right angles to the river so they acted as skids. He pushed one, Tikaani pushed the other and the raft splashed into the shallows.

The boys scrambled onto it and immediately their weight pushed the floats under. The raft bobbed but hardly any water water splashed onto the tarpaulin. Tikaani knelt and clutched the wood. The raft felt very vulnerable as it slowly began to spin out into the centre of the river. It trembled whenever one of them moved.

Beck had been expecting the random movement and was a little more relaxed. 'Comfortable?' he asked.

'Yeah, just about . . .'

'OK, tie the rucksacks to the frame. There's not much space and we could easily kick one of them over.'

'Right,' Tikaani agreed, maybe thinking of all the time and effort spent carrying those rucksacks this far. 'That would be kind of a waste . . .'

Beck dug the pole into the bottom of the river and pushed. The raft steadied a little and moved with the current.

Tikaani tied the second rucksack down and relaxed. 'How about a bird for the raft's name? Do you get albatrosses in Alaska?' he asked. 'The *Albatross* would be cool.'

'But albatrosses aren't meant to ever touch land.'

'Whoa! OK, not that . . .'

'How about the *Bar-tailed Godwit*?' Beck suggested, not seriously. He had seen that bird in a book and the name had stuck in his memory.

Tikaani pulled a mock scowl. 'You're really not taking this seriously.' His face lit up. 'The *Ptarmigan*! That's the state bird of Alaska.'

Beck smiled. 'OK, we'll pay our respects to Alaska.'

He knelt at the edge of the raft and pushed again with the pole to counter the spinning. It moved further into the river and started to turn the other way. The different lengths of the floats made it lean slightly. Finding their balance would be hard.

'Done.' Tikaani patted the nearest log. 'I name you the *Ptarmigan*.'

Beck gave the pole another nudge. It was like punting. You gave the raft a push and then used the pole as a rudder. But the best way was to let the current do the work. Let the raft find its own stability. He would use the pole to keep the raft centre-stream but not to drive it. Otherwise they would spin all the way to the sea.

The two boys and the *Ptarmigan* drifted down the Kynak towards Anakat.

It had been the right idea, Beck decided. He kept an eye on the bank. They were moving faster than a walking pace. Even allowing for the time taken to build the *Ptarmigan*, they would soon be ahead.

It wasn't a completely smooth ride. The raft wobbled more than a boat ever would. Every now and then a wave or a ripple threw another splash onto the deck, or water splattered against the underside of the tarpaulin.

But the sun was shining and its warmth reflected back off the deck. The lapping of the water was peaceful and soothing. Tikaani uncurled from his kneeling position and cautiously stretched himself out on the tarpaulin. Beck wasn't remotely surprised when his friend's eyes closed and it was obvious he was asleep. They were both worn out by their trek over the last three days. The only thing keeping them going was keeping going. Once they stopped moving, sleep soon caught up.

In fact, Beck could feel his own eyes getting heavy. Giving an occasional nudge with the pole didn't take much energy. He was having to raise his eyebrows just to keep his eyes open.

'OK,' he muttered. He dipped his hand in the river and splashed cold water in his face. 'Stay awake. Keep the mind working.' It seemed to have done the trick. His mind felt fresher, less cobwebby. But there seemed to be grit in his eyes. He blinked to clear them. Still gritty. He squeezed them shut . . .

* * *

A shock ran through Beck's body as the whole raft suddenly lurched. It was the kind of muscular spasm he sometimes got just before falling asleep.

And that meant he *had* been falling asleep.

Whoa! he thought. He looked around. The *Ptarmigan* was spinning again – Beck was facing the bank, which was still passing by at speed several metres away. They were still in the middle of the river. There weren't any distinguishing landmarks and he couldn't tell how long he had been asleep for. It probably hadn't been too long because he was still kneeling down and he still had the pole in his hands.

'OK. Wakey wakey, Beck Granger.' The first thing to do was straighten the *Ptarmigan* up again. He gave the pole a push against the bottom of the river.

Another jerk ran through the whole raft, though Beck was now wide awake. This time a wave of cold water splashed over Tikaani, who woke up with a yelp.

'Hey, that wasn't funny!'

'No, it wasn't,' Beck said grimly, and nodded ahead.

The river was no longer smooth. It rippled with waves and troughs. The *Ptarmigan* had just bounced through one of them. And up ahead, white foam seethed through the gaps between rocks jutting up out of the water.

The raft was heading straight for some rapids.

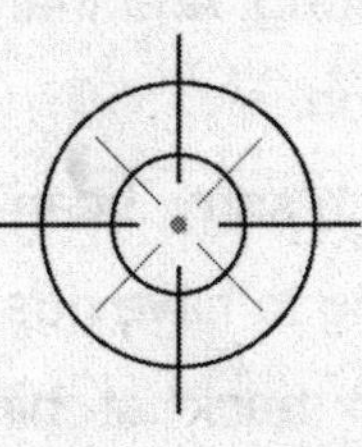

CHAPTER 36

Beck rammed the pole into the water and heaved with all his might. He probably had less than a minute to get them to the bank. Tikaani was kneeling up and staring at the rapids. He reminded Beck of a rabbit caught in the headlights of an oncoming car.

The raft moved towards the bank, but it also picked up speed towards the rapids. Beck swore and heaved again, and again. The bank grew tantalizingly close . . .

The pole hit something on the bottom of the river so hard that it was almost knocked from Beck's hands. The *Ptarmigan* moved maybe thirty centimetres to the left and a couple of metres further downstream. That settled it, Beck realized, his heart plummeting. He could steer but not push. The current was too strong. And that committed them to one course of action.

Beck swore. 'I'm sorry, I can't get us to the side in time. We're going to have ride the rapids.'

Tikaani looked back at him with wide-eyed, eloquent horror. The *Ptarmigan* dipped again and more water sloshed over them.

'OK,' his friend said bravely. 'What can I do?'

'Hold on!' Beck told him.

Tikaani nodded, got a grip on the raft and looked forwards again.

The rapids were dead ahead. The raft was bucking in the current and the rocks were almost upon them. Beck wanted to stick to the tongue of the rapids, where the most water was flowing, and keep away from dips where it swirled around the rocks, forming whirlpools. Taking a deep breath, he focused on where he wanted to go and thrust out with the pole. The *Ptarmigan* shot between two rocks on a smooth ramp of water, down into a boiling pool of white rage.

Water sluiced over the deck. If the rucksacks hadn't been tied down they would have been washed straight away. The raft surfaced like a submarine coming up for air. Both boys were gasping. The water felt icy as it streamed down their faces.

The raft heaved and bucked beneath them. Beck wiped the water from his eyes and looked around. They were surrounded by rocks and there was no obvious sign of the exit.

But the water knew where it was going and it took the *Ptarmigan* with it.

'We're going between those two!' Tikaani shouted, pointing to a gap that looked only a little wider than the raft.

Beck could see that the water seemed to dip down on the left. Time to stick to the right!

The raft curved round under Beck's guidance. One of the floats thumped into the rock on the right and the whole structure jarred. Beck winced. If something had to hit the solid lump of rocks, then he would rather it was that than fragile human bodies, but the *Ptarmigan* had to hold together. He had made it as solid as he could but he hadn't had this kind of treatment in mind.

The raft spun round as it fell and plunged backwards into the next pool, Beck's end first. It was a steep drop. The leading edge went under and kept going. Beck looked up and saw the rest of the raft rising above him. Tikaani was clinging on for dear life as tons of water threatened to push his end over. They were about two seconds away from capsizing.

'Hold on!' Beck shouted. He dropped the steering pole and scrambled up towards Tikaani. His extra weight helped push the top of the raft down again. A solid wave washed over the two boys, but the *Ptarmigan* stayed the right way up.

The pole was bobbing in the foam next to them. Beck grabbed at it and pulled it back in. The raft was spinning again. There was no way of telling which way was forwards, which way back. All Beck could do was fend them off the rocks that loomed in their way.

'I think . . . I think we're through . . .' Tikaani gasped. Beck spared a glance for the way they were going. His friend was right. The water was still rough but they seemed to be through the worst of the drops. Rocks and boulders still lay in their path but the route through was clear. The raft shot between them as if eager to get away. It kicked beneath them like a speedboat. Beck steered again, keeping to where the water looked deepest, steering away from several final holes, and the sound of the rapids receded behind them. They were shaken, and soaking wet, but they were safe.

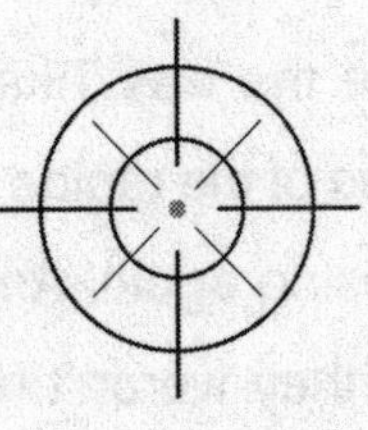

CHAPTER 37

Tikaani let out a whoop of triumph. Beck joined in, but not quite so eagerly. He had felt the raft shift under them when it crashed into the rocks. He lifted up a corner of the tarpaulin to look at the nearest tie. It was looser than it had been. The raft's whole frame was weakened.

'We need to get to the bank,' he said. 'We need to dry out . . .'

He was already pushing with the pole, but the water was still moving too fast. It was like it had been before the rapids. He could steer from side to side but the speed of the current always undid his work. Well, it didn't matter that much. The current would die down more and more the further they went, and then he could steer properly again.

'Uh, Beck . . .'

Beck didn't like the way Tikaani's voice rose as he spoke. The noise of the rapids had been dwindling – but now it was rising again. And since they hadn't turned round and they weren't heading back to the rapids behind them, that could only mean . . .

With a sinking feeling, Beck craned his neck to find out what Tikaani could see.

For a heart-stopping moment he thought that he was wrong; that there weren't any rapids at all. He couldn't see any rocks or any broken water . . .

And then the truth dawned. There weren't any rapids ahead because the river simply fell away. They were heading straight for a waterfall.

Various options flicked through Beck's head at lightning speed. They could bail out and swim for the bank. No – at the speed the water was moving, they would probably be swept over the falls anyway. They could stay in the raft and hope it bore the brunt of their fall. No, it might well land on top of them and pin them under. They would simply be battered to death on the rocks at the base of the falls and the raft would be smashed to pieces.

And that was it. No more ideas. So, since everything was impossible, Beck had to decide what was the least impossible and go for that.

He started to push the *Ptarmigan* towards the bank again. They could maybe get close enough to jump and swim for it, without being swept to their deaths.

Or . . .

Hope surged within him. On the left-hand bank he saw a fallen tree overhanging the side of the river. Its branches drooped down, almost dragging in the water. It must have fallen down quite recently, during the winter; it hadn't had the chance to decay. It might be their salvation.

'I'm heading for that,' he instructed Tikaani. 'We'll go under it and grab the branches.'

Tikaani had already seen the tree and nodded vigorously. 'Got you!'

'Untie the rucksacks and put yours on . . .'

They had barely a minute to get ready. Tikaani scrabbled at the knots he had tied, but eventually the rucksacks were loose. He pulled his on and knelt at the front of the raft, ready and poised. Beck spent the time making sure the raft was exactly aligned. He couldn't steer and climb at the same time. The water had to carry them right under the tree without suddenly taking them off to one side.

At the last moment he dropped the steering pole and shrugged his own rucksack on over his shoulders. And then they were under the branches.

Tikaani leaped for the nearest one and the whole tree seemed to sag under his weight. He shouted in alarm and his feet dragged against the deck of the raft. Beck scrambled forward and seized his friend's thighs, propelling him up. Damp leaves scraped against his face, as if the tree was trying to push him back into the river. Tikaani grabbed for a higher branch and pulled. Beck managed to push one of Tikaani's knees over the branch so that he was lying flat on it, out of the raft.

But the *Ptarmigan* had already passed under the tree. Now Beck had to clamber back to the rear of the raft to get a branch for himself. He could see just the one he wanted, a branch next to Tikaani's that looked strong enough to take his weight. He leaped for it—

And pain jabbed into his shoulder. A smaller branch that he hadn't seen through the leaves had pushed into him, holding him back. He fell back onto the raft, which wallowed beneath him.

'Beck!' Tikaani shouted.

Beck scrambled to his feet, waving his arms for balance. But, sickeningly, he knew that the branch was now just out of reach. He couldn't even jump for it.

He dropped to his knees again to balance the raft. His eyes met Tikaani's and saw only despair. Then the raft was swept down the river, Beck still on board, Tikaani safe and helpless on his branch. Beck turned away from his friend to face the edge of the falls.

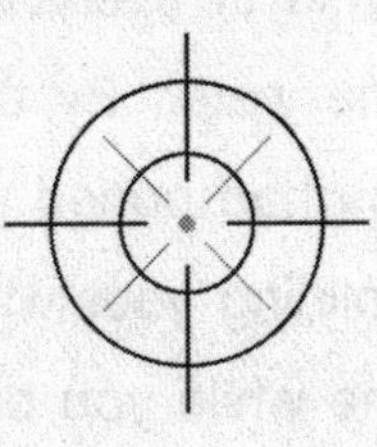

CHAPTER 38

All the previous options ran through Beck's mind again, but he knew there was only one real choice. The absolute priority was to *not* go over the falls. And there was no way he could stop the *Ptarmigan* doing exactly that. His chances were better *off* the raft than on.

And so he ditched the rucksack – it would only hold him back – and dived into the river. Hands above his head, feet together, he entered the water as cleanly as an Olympic swimmer. He was swimming for his life before he even broke the surface again.

Back at school Beck had always been good at the crawl. But he had never before needed to win a race quite so badly. His body fell straight into a rhythm. You breathed in every time your left arm came up out of the water. By the time it had hit the water again you had buried your face beneath the surface, streamlining your whole body like the bow of a submarine while you breathed out again and the water flowed over you. You stroked with your right arm, up and down, and then the left arm was coming up again and the cycle repeated itself. *Stroke-stroke-breathe-stroke-stroke-breathe* . . .

But Beck had felt the river pulling at him the moment he entered the water. It seemed that every cell of his body wanted to head down towards the falls. He knew he was making more progress in that direction than he was towards the bank. He was blinded by the water flowing over his face but he could make out that much. He was kicking with his feet but his heavy boots hampered him. All he had to propel him was the strength of his arms.

And then a wave washed over him; he was completely submerged, and this time there was no coming up. A new current seized hold of him. It had been lurking beneath the surface, ready for him, and it was twice as strong as the current above. He felt it whisk him away while his body twisted and turned, trying to head back to the air again.

Water roared in his ears and he had no idea which way was up or down. In theory, he knew, the thing to do was blow out some bubbles. Air always knew which was up and the bubbles would rise. But that depended on you being able to *see* the bubbles. All Beck could see was confused shades of light and dark, and he really didn't want to waste any of the precious air in his lungs.

Something slammed into him and he cried out in pain. His shout gurgled in his ears. That was half his air gone anyway. But Beck knew it could only be a rock, and rocks were stable. They didn't get swept away by the current. He tried hard to cling onto it, but already the water was pulling him away. He felt himself scrape along more rocks and then suddenly he was out in the air again, coughing and spluttering.

Beck spat the water out of his mouth and breathed in so deeply that the air whistled. The water pitched and heaved around him but there was a rock right by him and he could cling onto it. Gradually he took in his surroundings.

The current was just as strong. It still dragged at him. Even hanging onto the rock, he was making a bow wave. The roar of the falls was deafening – they were just a couple of metres away. So why wasn't he being swept over? Because, he realized, a semicircle of boulders stuck out from the side of the river, right on the edge of the falls. Water swirled into a little whirlpool there, and he had been swept in with it.

And if he wasn't very careful, he would be swept out again too. He tried to adjust his grip on the slippery rock and almost lost it altogether. *Oops!* Beck realized he wasn't going to get anywhere as long as he stayed in the water. All he could hope to do was climb out.

He glanced up as he clung on. The banks were a couple of metres high. Well, he could climb that high if he could get to them.

He gripped the rock and heaved with his arms, while his feet scrabbled against the side. But his boots could find no grip and he fell painfully against the sharp edges. He tried again, and again the current almost swept him away.

Beck lay against the side of the rock and made himself breathe calmly. He could do this. Before the cold of the river gave him hypothermia, before his strength gave out and he was swept away and dashed to pieces at the bottom of the falls, he could do this . . . if he could just work out how . . .

'Hey! Beck!' a familiar voice called. At the same time something hard hit him on the head. 'Whoa! Sorry . . .'

Beck looked round and almost had his eye poked out. The tip of a branch was waving right in front of his face. He looked towards the far end of the branch.

Tikaani was lying on his front, on the river bank, reaching out as far as he could safely go. And he was holding the branch out to Beck.

'You'd better take it,' Tikaani called, his voice rising with buried panic, ''cos I don't know how long I can hold on here . . .'

Beck didn't hesitate and grabbed the branch for all he was worth.

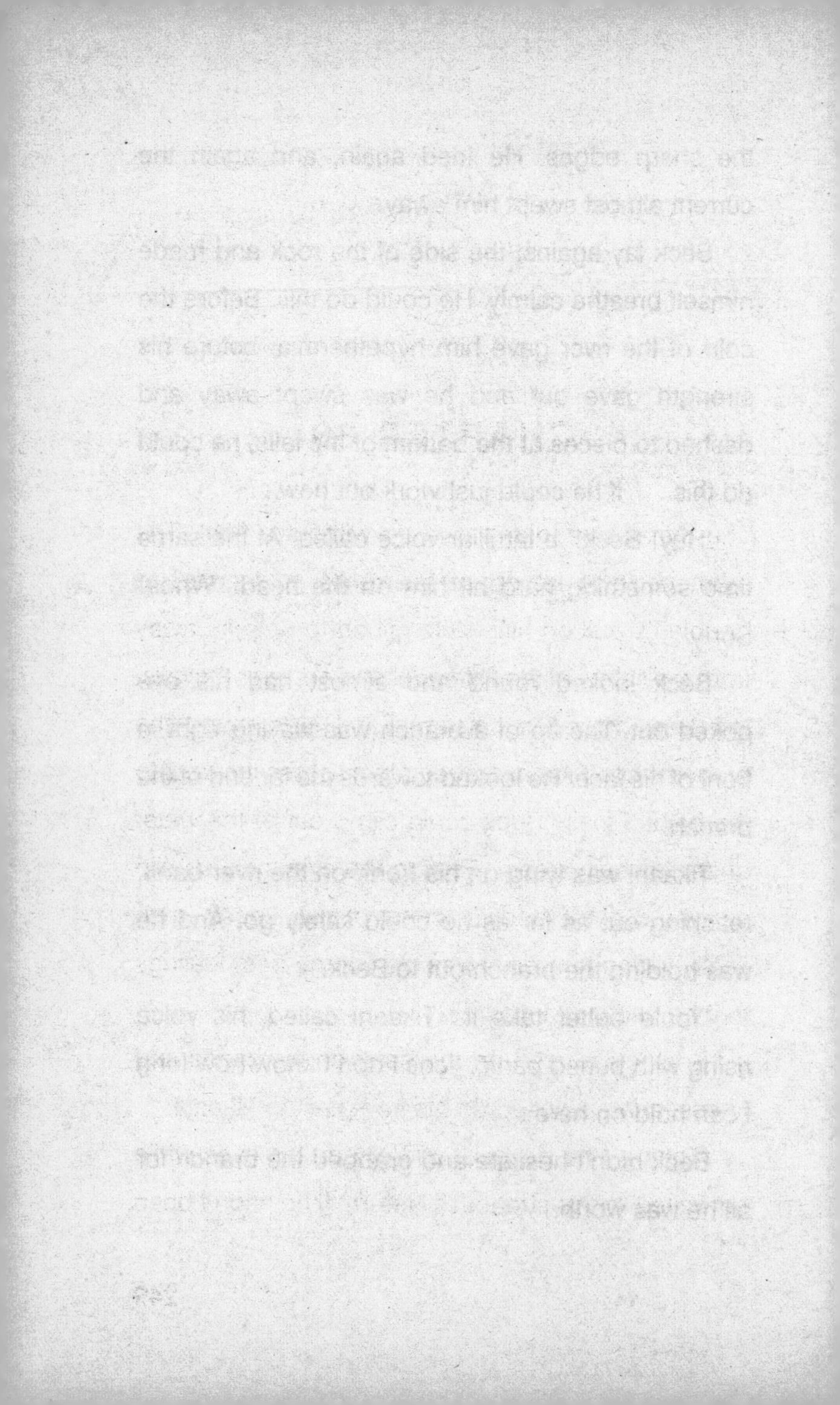

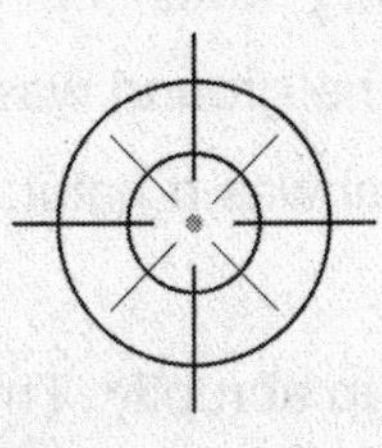

CHAPTER 39

The Kynak river didn't give up without a fight. The moment Beck let go of the rocks, it seemed to double its pull on him, determined to get him away from the safety of the little pool and out over the falls. But Beck wrapped his arms and legs round the branch while Tikaani dragged him across the pool to the bank. Finally Beck could climb out of the water under his own steam. Feeling the river's clutch slip away down his body – chest, waist, knees, then finally letting him go – was one of the best feelings that he had ever known.

Beck clambered up the bank on his hands and knees, and collapsed on his front next to Tikaani.

'Thanks,' he gasped, and closed his eyes while he waited for his strength to return. If he hadn't been drenched in freezing water, he would have been pleasantly warm. The ground was dry, the sun was shining, and Tikaani was a natural wind break. But Beck shivered.

'Sorry.' He sat up abruptly. 'I'm going to have to strip off and get dry.'

'Hey, fair enough,' said Tikaani with a shrug, and a grin that was only slightly malicious. Maybe he was remembering being pushed over in the snow. 'I'll see if there's anything dry.'

And so, while Beck ran on the spot and did push-ups and star jumps, Tikaani rummaged through his rucksack. Almost everything in it was damp, but not as soaked as Beck. It had never gone fully underwater. Neither had Tikaani. His hair and trousers were dripping wet but he had been wearing a waterproof coat as they went down the rapids. His torso was mostly dry, and warm.

Tikaani changed his trousers and socks and chose the least damp clothes he could find for Beck. He wrung out the wet clothes as best he could and went to stand on the edge of the falls while Beck got dressed again. Beck could feel a healthy warm glow inside him now. It didn't matter if the clothes were a little damp. The wind wasn't strong enough to chill them. If they could just get walking again, then their own bodies would generate enough warmth to dry the clothes properly.

And that, Beck thought sourly, was about the only good news he could think of. He had almost got them killed. They had lost the tarpaulin with the raft. They had lost his rucksack, which contained the map and his water bottle and half their clothes—

'Hey, Beck!' Tikaani was walking towards him and pointing back at the falls with his thumb. 'Pujortok!'

'If that's an Anak word meaning "Life almost ended here",' Beck muttered, 'you've got that right . . .'

'No.' Tikaani seemed strangely cheerful. 'It's an Anak word meaning "It smokes", and it's what we call this waterfall. I've been here before.'

Beck blinked. 'You have?'

'We only got as far as the bottom, so I didn't recognize it for a moment from up here. My dad took me hiking . . .'

It was like Tikaani was suddenly talking an alien language. Beck understood the words but his brain just couldn't process them to make sense. '*You* have been *hiking*?'

'Well, yeah.' Tikaani shrugged. 'I mean, we stayed in a tent and we ate food out of cans and we had sleeping bags and we didn't feel cold or hungry once . . . And did I mention we drove out here in a truck? But technically, I've been hiking. And I'm pretty sure we can be in Anakat by sunset!'

The waterfall poured down a twenty-metre cliff. They had to go some distance away from the river for the sharp drop to even out enough for them to climb down. Seeing them from the side, Beck could understand how the falls got their name. The glittering spray of falling water billowed and swelled in the breeze like wood smoke before drifting off over the top of the fir trees. A rainbow arced through the spray from the top to the bottom, its curve pointing the way they had to go.

By the time they reached the foot of the cliff, Beck's mood was much better than it had been at the top. His good humour was fully restored when they found, clinging to the slope at the bottom of the falls, a bush with the largest collection of lingonberries they had ever seen. They set off along the lower reaches of the Kynak with full stomachs, warm bodies and light hearts.

Tikaani was in a talkative mood and Beck was happy to let him chat. He felt just as optimistic as his friend but his immersion in the river had taken more out of him than he had realized. He shot a sideways look at the Kynak beside them, now so calm and peaceful as Pujortok receded behind them. He wasn't going to trust that river again in a hurry.

And meanwhile he let Tikaani talk.

'My granddad says it was a great moment in a boy's life, the first time he went out on a hunt. The boys from the village would be taken out here for a few days . . .'

All Tikaani's buried Anak memories seemed to be floating to the surface, jogged loose by their experiences of the last couple of days. Most of them were handed-down memories from his grandfather.

'Some soldiers came up here for a training

course. Granddad set some snares overnight and in the morning they'd caught a couple of hares. So they skinned them and cooked them and tried to give them to the soldiers, but they wouldn't touch them because Granddad had handled the meat with his bare hands . . . Hey!' Tikaani paused and looked around. He glanced back at the mountains and took in their surroundings: the river, a bit of high ground to one side. He seemed to be taking mental bearings.

'We're almost at the clearing where we camped,' he said happily. 'We could rest there.'

Beck nodded wearily. Rest would be good. Just a quick one, before the final push on to Anakat.

The clearing wasn't far. It was fifty metres across with a soft floor of pine needles that made Beck want to throw himself down and sleep. The sun was high enough to shine down into it and the fir trees all around kept out the wind. It was perfect in every way.

Row-rrr-or!

Beck's blood turned to ice. Had he imagined—

'Ah!' Tikaani burst out laughing. 'They're so cute!'

A pair of bear cubs tumbled out from behind a bush. Their fur was brown and soft, so fine it could have been shampooed specially. Brown fur, Beck thought despairingly; that made them grizzlies. Their faces were round and friendly, each with a pair of circular ears perched comically on top. They wrestled together, somersaulting across the pine needles, nipping each other playfully.

Beck kicked himself. He had forgotten one of the prime rules. He had been too tired to think straight and distracted by the false security of assuming they were near Anakat. The prime rule was: *Look out for bears!*

'You know about bears! We're getting out of here now!'

'Well, yeah, but . . . they're not so fierce!' Tikaani protested.

And that was when something large, heavy and angry burst out of the bushes behind them. The boys reluctantly looked round.

'No,' Beck agreed, 'but *she* is . . .'

The cubs' fur was fine but the mother grizzly's was brown and shaggy, tipped with silver. The cubs looked soft and cuddly, but muscles like steel cable rippled beneath the mother's pelt. The cubs were just playing but the mother was seriously wired about the two little mammals daring to stand between her and her children.

The cubs were the size of a large dog. The mother reared up onto her hind legs and was suddenly way taller than a man. Two and a half metres and half a ton of bear roared its anger at the boys. And then she dropped onto all fours again and charged.

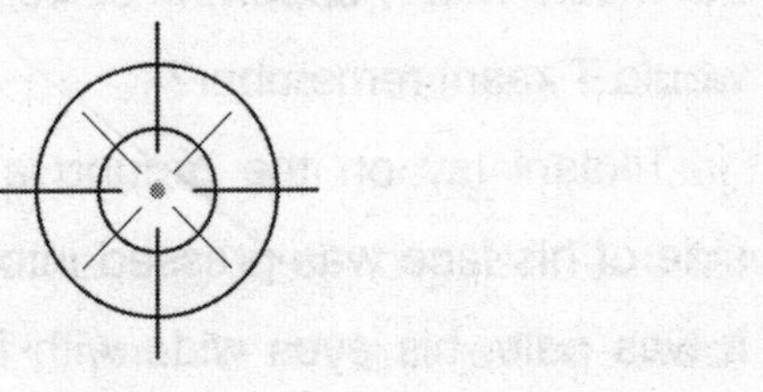

CHAPTER 40

Tikaani screamed and turned to run. Beck grabbed him and held him back.

'Lie down!' he snapped. He flung himself to the ground and dragged Tikaani down next to him. 'Just play dead!'

The most dangerous place you could ever be with a bear, Beck knew, was between a mother and her cubs. They do whatever they can to annihilate the threat and protect their young. With its metre-long strides a grizzly would catch even a running human in seconds. Your only hope is to play dead.

He tried to remember – how long ago had he told Tikaani about bears? It had been when they were setting off from the plane. Just a couple of days. But so much had happened since then. How much would Tikaani remember?

Tikaani lay on the ground a metre away. The side of his face was pressed into the pine needles: it was pale, his eyes wide with fear. Beck realized he was lying on his front; he himself had curled up into a tight ball, giving himself as much protection as he could. He hadn't reminded Tikaani of that and couldn't take the risk now. If the bear saw him move, she would toss him about like a rag doll.

'Even if she prods you or roughs you up a bit,' Beck hissed, 'don't move. Just lie there.' Tikaani didn't nod but Beck saw the understanding in his terrified eyes.

Beck knew his advice was much easier said than done, but it was all they could do.

The bear loomed over them. Her shadow blotted out the sun.

A leg as thick as a tree branch crunched into the ground between them. Pine needles and insects clung onto the thickly matted fur and the animal smell was overwhelming. Then the leg was lifted up again as the bear moved on. Beck could sense her circling round them.

Suddenly Tikaani was jerked back out of Beck's sight. Beck bit his lip, wanting to cry out for his friend. But Tikaani stayed silent and Beck guessed the bear had only dug a claw into his rucksack to see what would happen. Tikaani was unhurt. He didn't move and he didn't make a sound.

The bear stepped over the prone boy and lowered her head to examine Beck. *Whuff*. Her nostrils flared as she breathed in and out again. Her breath was like a pair of bellows. Beck lay completely still. He wondered if the bear could hear his pounding heart. To him it sounded like a drum-and-bass mix.

The bear put out a claw and nudged him, like Beck would prod a spider in the bath. Beck resisted all his instincts and lay as still as he could. The bear's lips drew back, revealing just a hint of her yellow fangs. She nudged him again with a low growl, trying to provoke a reaction. Beck determinedly played dead.

The great head darted forward and she seized

the sleeve of his jacket in her front teeth, missing his skin by half an inch. Beck didn't move. His chest grew tight and he realized that he was holding his breath. He wondered if he could let it out and take another without the bear noticing. Then she shook her head and Beck shook with her, his sleeve still held firmly in her mouth. He couldn't help it. He gasped, and when she dropped him he put out a hand to break his fall. Immediately, cursing himself, he lay as flat as he could on the ground, trying to be even more limp than before. Had the bear noticed him move? Would she take it as a challenge?

She put her nose to the side of his head and growled. Her breath, hot and smelling of rotten meat, washed over him. Beck closed his eyes and waited in despair for the bite.

The gale of foul breath stopped suddenly. Beck could picture the bear drawing her head back, jaws opening, preparing to lunge.

But still nothing happened. There was a sudden sense of emptiness next to him. Beck half opened one eye, then the other. The bear was gone.

She was already over on the other side of the

clearing, moving with an astonishing lightness of foot over the pine needles. She had obviously decided the boys were not a threat. She shepherded the cubs away with another growl, which Beck translated as: *What have I told you before about playing with humans?*

And then mother and cubs were gone.

The boys stayed exactly where they were for a few minutes more, Tikaani taking his lead from Beck. Finally, when Beck was absolutely sure the bears weren't coming back, he sat up. Tikaani did the same. They exchanged a look. Then, without a word, they got up and headed out of the clearing.

'Character forming,' Beck said after a while.

'Trouser staining,' said Tikaani with feeling.

Beck picked up a small fallen branch and whacked it hard against the nearest tree. 'Coming through!' he called into the woods. 'Just ignore us!'

And so, talking loudly and making plenty of noise as a warning to any unsuspecting bears, they headed on towards Anakat.

* * *

'I'd do the same,' Tikaani said suddenly, about half an hour later.

Beck looked at him quizzically. 'The same as what?'

Tikaani jerked a thumb back over his shoulder. 'The same as Ma Bear back there. Like, that clearing was her kids' playroom. Wouldn't you be ticked off if two strangers just came into your home?'

'I'd express my irritation,' Beck agreed with a straight face.

'It's her home,' Tikaani pressed on. Then, more quietly and with a hint of wonder, he repeated: 'It's her home. Who has the right to just walk into someone's *home*?'

Beck looked at him with respect. This wasn't just chatter. He sensed anger behind Tikaani's words. He wondered if it was aimed at Lumos Petroleum.

He hadn't thought of the petrol company in days. They'd had other things on their mind, like survival. But ultimately, none of this would have happened if it wasn't for Lumos. As they got closer to Anakat, the company was making a comeback into his awareness.

'No one,' he said.

'No one,' Tikaani agreed. And again he repeated it, to himself. 'No one.'

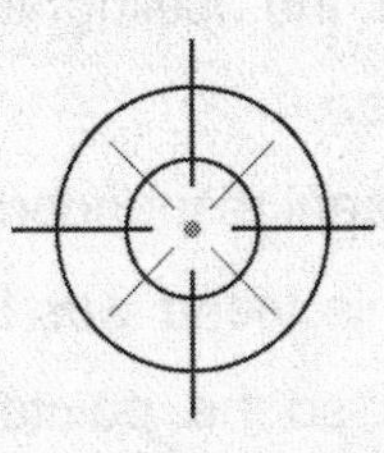

CHAPTER 41

They saw no more bears, but at one point Beck did see something else through the trees – a fleeting shadow, hugging the ground, loping along easily, parallel to their route. He almost laughed. 'So you made it too . . .' he murmured to himself.

Their old friend the wolf phantom had rejoined them.

Or was it their old friend? Maybe this part of Alaska was just full of wolves that liked to trot along on their own. It didn't seem likely, though it was more probable than a wolf following them all the way from the plane crash – including fording the river, crossing the mountains, spending the night in a blizzard and following them on a raft. But Beck couldn't shake off the feeling that the wolf was making a journey too.

'Say again,' Tikaani responded.

Beck decided his friend was hardened enough to the wilderness, so he pointed. 'I could have sworn—'

He stopped. The wolf had gone and Tikaani was looking at him very strangely.

'Nothing,' Beck muttered. 'How much further to Anakat?'

'We're here,' Tikaani said, and without any warning the trees parted.

It took a moment to sink in.

They were beside an inlet that wound its way in from the sea, with steep slopes of earth and rock. It opened out into a wider bay, and there, further down the slope, on the shore, was Anakat.

Beck wasn't quite sure what he had expected. The way Tikaani spoke of it, he had almost imagined a community of traditional caribou-skin tents and campfires. Anakat wasn't *quite* that far behind. You could keep to traditional ways, Beck reckoned, and still have a reasonable degree of comfort. If a wooden house kept you warmer than a skin tent or an igloo, then you lived in a wooden house. If electric lights were easier to see by than burning oil lamps, then you used electric lights. The Anak picked and chose from the modern world, but they didn't let it rule them. They took only what would best help them live their traditional life at this high, cold latitude.

Anakat was a scattering of wooden buildings. They looked a little like giant toy houses – simple rectangles with steep, pointed roofs to shed the snow in winter. They were built on low stone pilings to keep them off the cold ground and painted in weathered shades of red and green and blue. That was the only ornamentation. This wasn't the kind of village where you bothered to keep up with the neighbours. The roads between them were dirt and gravel. By the water's edge, Beck could make out the dark silver forms of fish hung up on smoking racks. The community's boats bobbed at a small jetty and Beck could see a couple of canoes cutting their way through the waves.

The boys trudged down the slope towards the

village. A strange roaring in Beck's ears made him put his head on one side thoughtfully. What was that? It wasn't the wind. It wasn't the sea lapping against the rocks. It wasn't any mechanical sound, or any sound of the modern world . . .

And then, as they approached Anakat, he realized. It wasn't any modern sound. It wasn't any sound at all. No motor cars. No music. No aircraft. It had been just the same in the wilderness, of course, but Beck was used to leaving all that behind when he returned to civilization.

Not this time. Anakat was a scene of timeless peace. Apart from the battered station wagon parked outside one house – and the satellite dish on the side – it could have been any time in the last two hundred years.

'That's the airstrip,' Tikaani said, pointing across the inlet. On the far side, at the end of a wooden bridge, the land was flat and an orange windsock billowed in the breeze. 'Where we *would* have arrived. And this . . . is home.'

Home was the house with the wagon and the dish. It was another of the giant toy houses, plain and unadorned – no kind of porch or balcony. The steps that led up to the entrance were a pair of concrete blocks. The door was firmly shut and the windows sat squarely in their frames. It might have been made of wood, using techniques a couple of centuries old, but Beck was prepared to bet the house was less draughty and more snug than many modern homes further south.

The door opened and a woman stepped out. She wore jeans and a red check coat. She was talking frantically to someone behind her, still in the house, and not looking where she was going.

'Tell him to keep trying on the radio . . .'

She turned round and stopped when she saw them, shock stamped onto her broad face.

'Hey.' Tikaani suddenly seemed abashed. His hand twitched in a half-wave. 'Hi, Mom.'

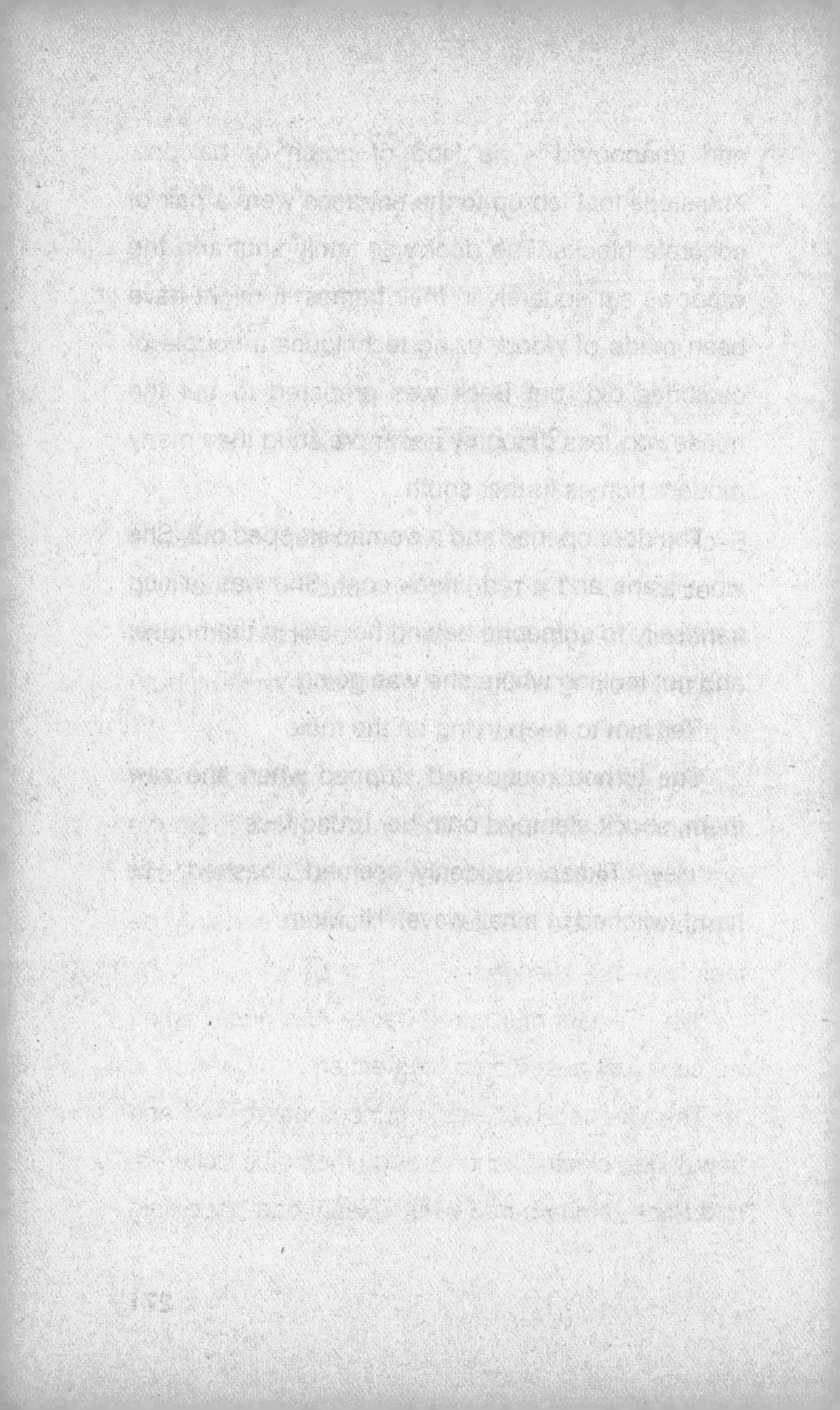

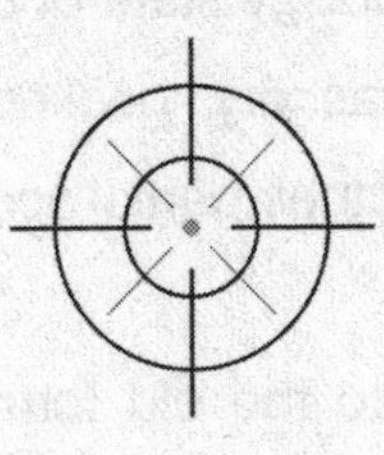

CHAPTER 42

Beck looked out at the sea of faces in Anakat's meeting hall. The building was packed. About two hundred heads were turned towards him and Tikaani, their distinctly Inuit features somehow both impassive and eager.

'Couldn't we just put up a notice?' Beck murmured to his friend. This wasn't going to be the first time they had told their story and would quite probably not be the last. But it would certainly be their largest audience.

'No,' Tikaani murmured back. 'And guess what, we can't just post it on a blog either . . .'

The wooden hall was a curious mix of old and new. It had electric light – though the bulbs flickered, and Beck remembered what Tikaani had once said about the slightly dodgy state of the generator. The floor of the hall was dry, packed earth. This was another example of their partial accommodation with the modern world.

They still kept to the old forms in many ways. Once, Beck presumed, the people of Anakat would have gathered around a large fire for these meetings. Right now they all sat in circular rows, all staring towards the centre of the room where Tikaani's dad, the headman of Anakat, was speaking. Beck and Tikaani sat behind him.

There had been time to eat and shower and change into fresh clothes of Tikaani's. There had *not* been time to do what Beck wanted to do most: sleep.

It had all happened very quickly after they'd arrived at Tikaani's home. It had taken thirty seconds to deliver the gist of the message: Al hurt, needing help, at these coordinates. Tikaani's dad had got onto the satellite phone – Anakat's best way of staying in touch with the outside world, apart from a dodgy radio link – before they finished.

He was talking to someone in Bethel, which Beck remembered was the nearest large town, about a hundred miles further up the coast.

Tikaani was hugged to death by his mother while Beck stood by and wondered vaguely what it must be like to have parents to come home to. He got some idea when she let go of her son and pulled him into an embrace that squeezed the breath out of him. Meanwhile Tikaani was being smothered by a much older woman. She was shorter than him. Her long hair was white and her face was mostly smoothed-out wrinkles. She was introduced as Tikaani's grandmother. She shook Beck's hand and her features were split by a wide smile.

The satellite phone beeped while Tikaani's mum was fixing a quick meal of hot soup and rolls.

'That was Bethel,' said Tikaani's dad when he hung up. 'There's a helicopter with a doctor on board on its way to pick up your uncle.'

And with those words, Beck felt the adrenaline that had powered him ever since the crash . . . just go.

But they still needed to eat, so Beck and Tikaani

described their adventures between mouthfuls of rolls and soup.

They described fording the river, and Tikaani's misadventure in the frozen lake, and crossing the crevasse. At that point Tikaani's mum interrupted.

'The elders will have to hear of this,' she told his father.

He nodded proudly. 'Of course. But not before I've heard it first.'

Elders? Beck thought. He took it to mean they would have to repeat the whole thing to a bunch of boring old pensioners. At the time he hadn't known about the full town meeting. He had glanced wryly at Tikaani.

And Tikaani had just shrugged. *He* had known. 'You'll see . . .' he had said.

The boys continued their story, telling Tikaani's family about their increasing frustration at not being able to find the pass.

Tikaani's grandmother sat up straight and spoke for the first time. 'White Wolf Pass,' she said knowingly. Then, not asking but stating, 'It was Tikaani who found it.'

'Well, yes, he did,' Beck confirmed.

She nodded, and beamed. 'The wolves are the guardians of the mountains, Beck Granger. In the winter and spring when the snows are heavy, White Wolf Pass is the only way through, but only those favoured by the wolves find the way, for it is well hidden.'

'Um . . . yes. Right,' Beck agreed.

He remembered the wolf – wolves? – he had glimpsed, or thought he had glimpsed, on their journey. Yes, he could believe the wolves had favoured them. And escorted them, just to make sure.

He glanced again at Tikaani; Tikaani shot him a shy smile. Beck knew that, once – and only a few days ago at that – his friend would have scoffed at his grandmother's belief in the old ways and the old spirits. Only a few months ago, so would he. But he had learned the hard way about the spirits in Colombia, and now it had come home to Tikaani too. His friend had learned respect for the practicalities of his ancestors' traditional ways – the things that could keep you alive – and with them he had also absorbed a little of their faith.

But the biggest surprise was yet to come.

'Didn't I tell you, my son?' Now the old lady was talking to Tikaani's dad. 'When you named the boy, you asked who should be his guardian and I said—'

'Yes, Mother,' the man agreed with a patient smile. 'Yes, you did.'

Beck looked from one to the other, not understanding. Finally he looked at Tikaani for clarification.

'Tikaani means "wolf",' his friend mumbled round a mouthful of roll. 'Didn't I say?'

Beck gaped, then closed his mouth. 'No,' he managed eventually. 'You didn't.'

Tikaani shrugged and swallowed his roll. Then he leaned forward. 'In fact,' he added confidentially, 'a couple of times I swear that I saw a wolf, but I figured you had enough to worry about, so I didn't say a word . . .'

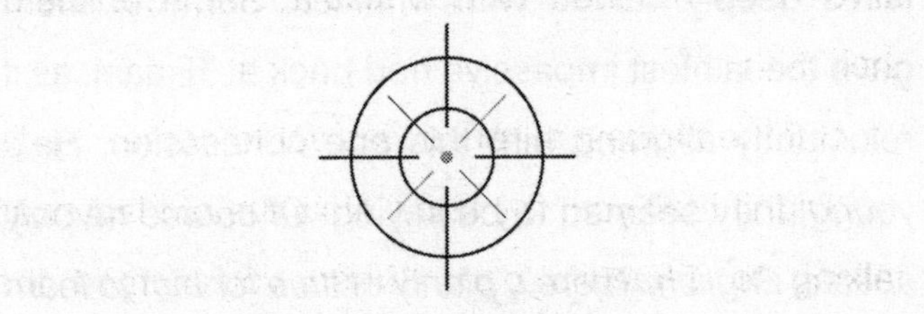

CHAPTER 43

Tikaani's dad was addressing the people inside the hall in a mixture of Anak and English. Finally he turned to the boys with a wide smile, and gestured that they should step forward and begin their telling. Tikaani put a hand on Beck's arm.

'It's OK. Let me.'

There was a strange note in Beck's friend's voice. Intrigued, Beck watched Tikaani step forward and raise his arms up.

'Tikaani, son of Kunuk, son of Panigoniak. Forgive me that I only speak the tongue of the Yankees.'

He said that last bit to the very front row, where the oldest men and women of the village sat. They had long grey hair, women and men alike, and flat faces deeply carved with wrinkles. Some of them gave the faintest impassive nod back at Tikaani, as if reluctantly allowing him this one concession. *He's young*, they seemed to be saying. *Of course he only speaks English. There's plenty of time for him to learn to do this properly.*

Tikaani launched into the story of their journey, from the moment the plane's engine had failed. Beck settled back in his chair. Tikaani had a clear gift for story-telling. He could convey the moment, the emotion of each situation they had faced together. There was a rhythm to his speech, a natural patter that just carried you along. It was like . . . Beck tried to think . . . it was like a song.

And suddenly Beck realized what was going on. Way back at the start of all this, the pilot had mentioned Anakat's oral tradition. This was it! Tikaani was reciting the latest instalment in the village's history. Their adventures were the latest chapter in an organic audio book that went back hundreds of years. This wasn't just a talk, it was a podcast; and those old people in the front row weren't just respected elders, they were the village's iPods.

Now Beck was captivated. He wondered if Tikaani had ever known he could do this. Born and bred in Anakat, and once determined to turn his back on the place; now he had fallen back into it as easily as a duck takes to water. This was their obligation to Anakat. The story had just happened around them as they left the plane and climbed the mountains and rafted down the river. Now it had to be spoken into the village's memory.

Then, maybe, Beck thought, they could sleep . . .

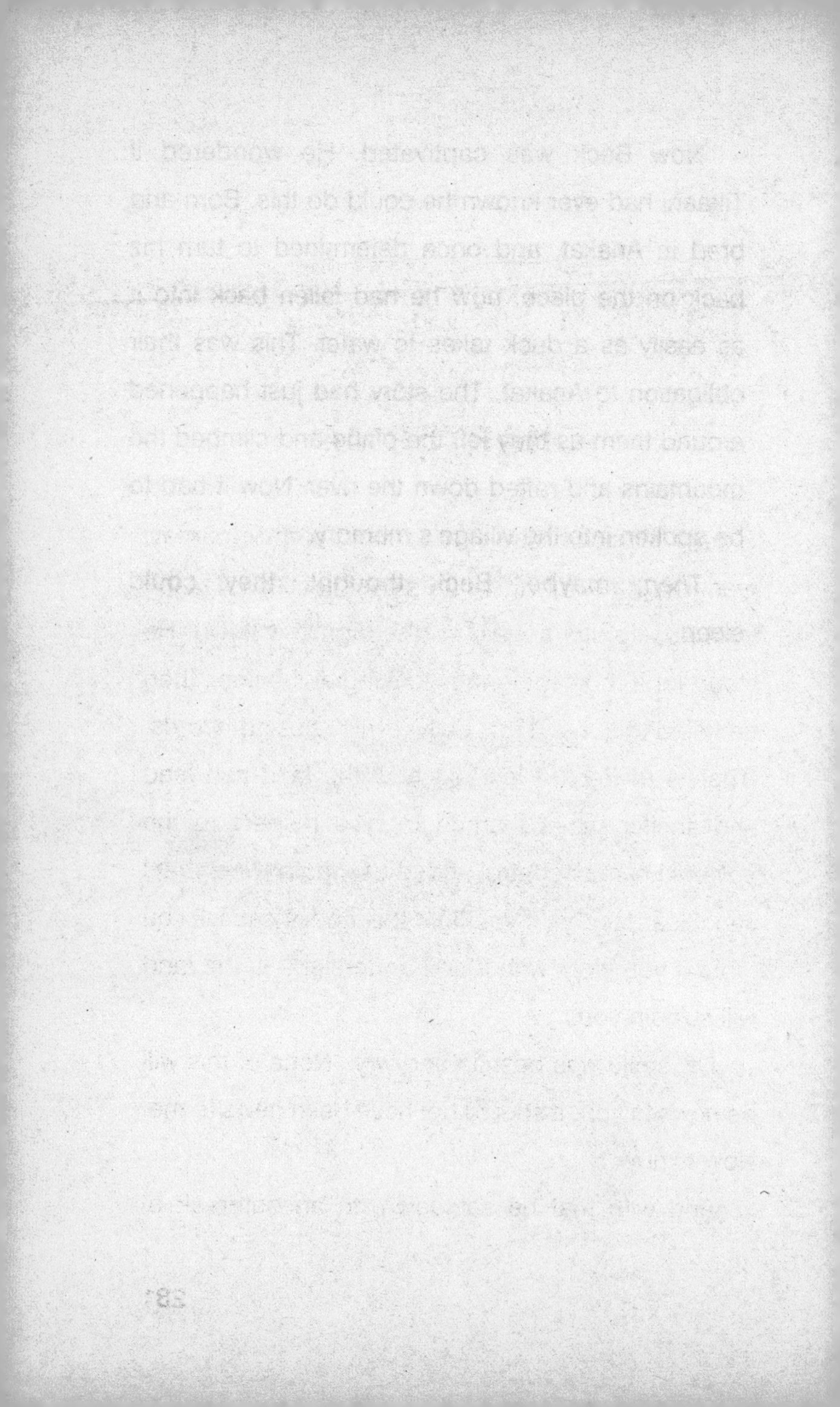

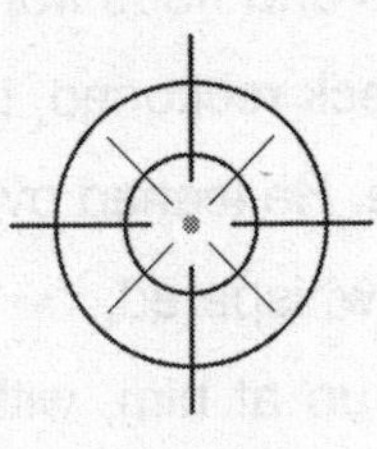

CHAPTER 44

Tikaani finished his straight account of their journey, reaching the point where the boys had arrived at the front door of his house, but he didn't sit down. He stood for a moment longer, looking at the floor, then he lifted his head to deliver his closing words. 'Thanks to Beck, I learned how the land can feed and shelter me. I learned to give respect to the powers I cannot control and to use the powers that I can. I learned that if you fight the land, it can kill you – but if you work with it and understand it, the land will sustain you.'

His smile was bashful and wry. 'None of this will be news to you. It should not have been news to me. Now I know.'

And with that he sat down, to an outbreak of

approving murmurs and nods from the villagers. By Anak standards, Beck reckoned, this was a wave of rapturous applause. He leaned over to Tikaani.

'Well done,' he whispered.

Tikaani looked up at him, with glistening eyes. 'Yeah. Thanks.'

Afterwards, Tikaani's family and the two boys walked slowly back to the house. It took a while because people kept coming up and shaking Beck and Tikaani's hands. Beck's feet were dragging on the gravel roads.

Sleep now! He thought. *Sleep, sleep, sleep* . . .

But first Tikaani's dad called Bethel again to check on the helicopter. He hung up and beamed at Beck.

'They've got Al and he's fine,' he said with a broad smile. 'In fact, he's so fine they've got time to swing by here and pick you up. They'll be here in about half an hour.'

The helicopter flew low over Anakat, hanging in the air like a giant metal wasp. Its engine rattled the windows in their frames.

Beck, Tikaani, Tikaani's parents and about half of Anakat made their way down to the foreshore where the helicopter was landing. The blast of its rotor whipped up sand and spray into a cloud that stung Beck's eyes. He hung back until he heard the change in pitch of its engine which meant that it was powering down. The rotor still scythed the air overhead but he ran forward, head lowered, and pulled open the cabin door.

And there was Uncle Al! He lay on a stretcher on the floor of the cabin, covered with blankets, and a paramedic fussed over him. A saline drip fed fluid into his arm and his face was pale, but there was no hiding the warmth of his smile.

'Beck!' His voice was barely loud enough to hear over the dying sound of the engine, but it didn't quaver. 'Tikaani too, of course. Thank you, boys, so much . . .'

But Beck was already hugging him, as best you can when a man is strapped into a stretcher.

The medic spoke. 'Two minutes.' He scowled at the boys. '*I* wanted to take him straight to hospital. He only got this diversion at all because he's paying for it.'

Two minutes! The boys looked at each other. They had gone through so much together to get here. Now Beck was about to be whisked away, just like that. It felt odd. It felt wrong. You shouldn't just disappear from a friend's life like that.

But of course . . .

'You'll be back.' Tikaani's smile was brave.

'Yeah.' Beck smiled wryly. 'Of course. I mean, we've still got to make that documentary, haven't we?'

'And those are my clothes you're wearing.'

'True. No other reason for coming back, really.'

Tikaani grinned. 'None at all!'

He squeezed Beck's hand and then backed out of the cabin and hurried away to join his parents. Beck strapped himself into a seat and peered out of the window. The pilot hopped out of the cockpit to slam the cabin door shut and check it was fastened. Then he clambered back in and the engine began to gather power again. Beck waved to his friend as the machine rose into the air and turned away from Anakat, over the inlet.

The land fell away beneath them. Village and

inlet merged into the endless cover of fir trees. The mountains that had done their best to kill Beck and Tikaani were just a picturesque backdrop. Everything gleamed in the golden sun and Beck felt his eyes grow heavy.

He didn't want to see Anakat go, but he blinked, and suddenly he had lost it. Where had it gone? It took a moment to locate the inlet again. The cluster of buildings was suddenly tiny. It must have been a long blink, he thought, and he could feel another coming on. Well, Beck told himself, you've got to blink, but make it a quick one . . .

And so he closed his eyes, and the next time he opened them they were circling the landing pad of Bethel's hospital.

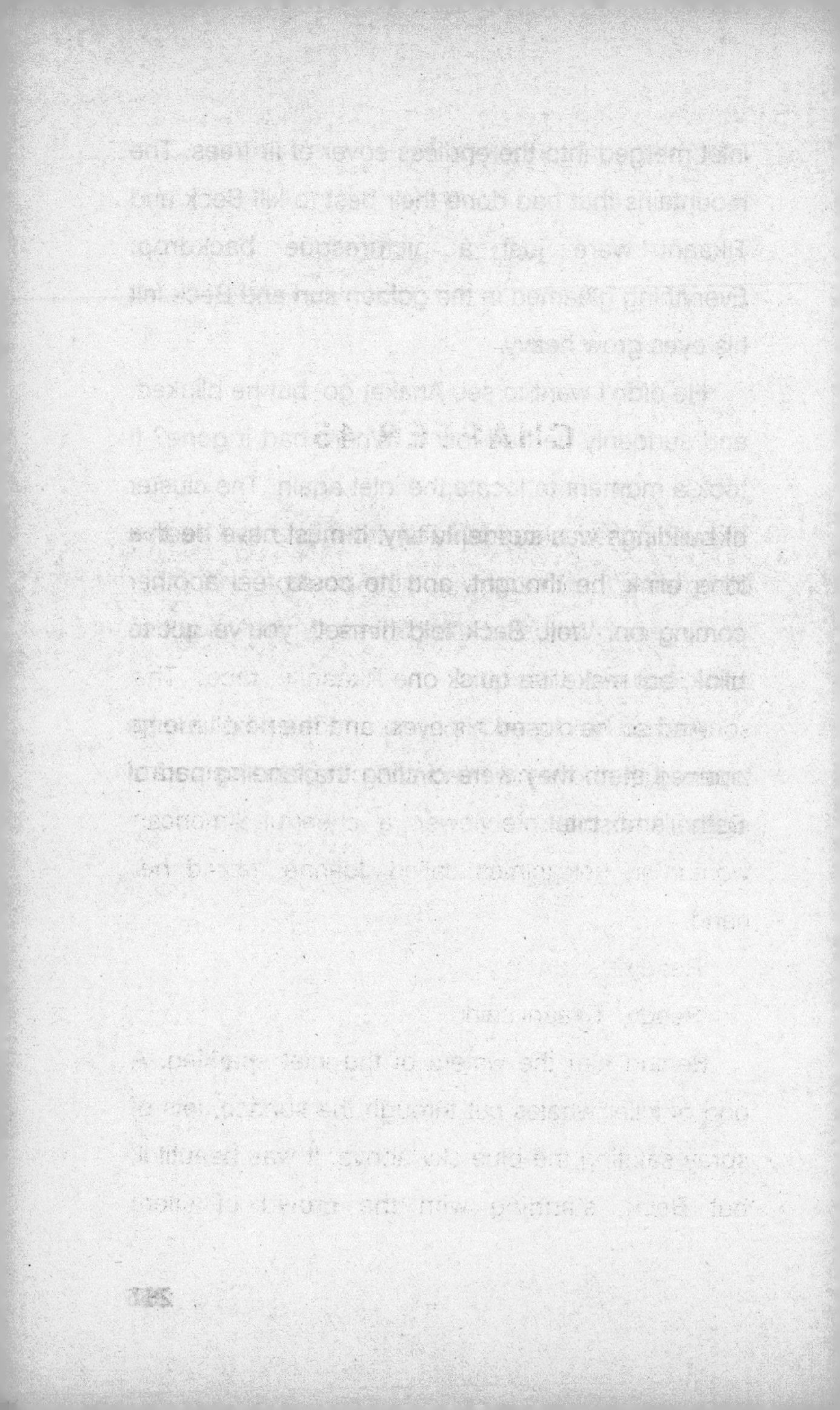

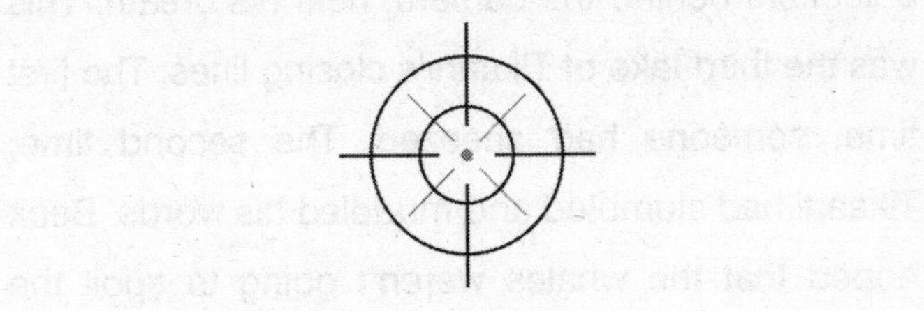

CHAPTER 45

Tikaani shifted uncomfortably from one foot to the other while the film crew got into position.

One man adjusted the camera on his shoulder and focused the lens on Tikaani's face. The sound man held a microphone on the end of a long boom, just above his head and out of the camera's sight. And the interviewer, a cheerful American woman in her thirties called Joanne, raised her hand.

'Ready?'

'Ready,' Tikaani said.

Behind him the waters of the inlet sparkled. A pod of killer whales cut through the surface, jets of spray saluting the blue sky above. It was beautiful, but Beck, standing with the crowd of silent onlookers behind the camera, held his breath. This was the third take of Tikaani's closing lines. The first time, someone had sneezed. The second time, Tikaani had stumbled and muddled his words. Beck hoped that the whales weren't going to spoil the shot. He had had no idea there was so much to a simple interview.

'And again . . . go.'

Tikaani beamed at the camera. 'I mean,' he said, 'you wouldn't break up a priceless painting because you wanted it for wood, would you?'

The words sounded a little stilted at first. Tikaani wasn't a natural actor. But then his genuine anger and passion started to shine through, creeping into his voice.

'So why' – he half turned, and with a wave of the hand indicated the inlet, and Anakat, and the wilderness beyond it – 'do the same here?'

He turned to face the camera again. 'There are alternative fuel sources. There's renewable energy. But this isn't renewable and once this is gone, it's gone for ever.'

'And cut!' Joanne said. 'Brilliant, Tikaani.

We'll use that. We can make the six o'clock news.'

Tikaani grinned, and sauntered over to Beck and Al. 'Hi, strangers.'

It had been a week since they'd seen each other face to face. It felt longer. They had talked on the phone – they had even been interviewed together in a conference call – but that was all. Beck hadn't realized how much he'd missed his friend.

'That was very good. Very good indeed,' said Al. He was no stranger to making programmes. Beck could see his uncle's words of praise meant a lot to Tikaani.

'Yeah, well, I've been getting practice . . .' he mumbled. 'Did you just get here? Was that you about ten minutes ago?'

Beck and Al had just flown in by helicopter. It hadn't been hard to find Tikaani. They had simply followed the line of TV crews.

'That was us,' Beck agreed, and Tikaani flashed his old grin.

'You interrupted me talking to CBS.'

'Well, gee,' said Beck. 'I *am* sorry.' They turned towards the village, Al limping on his stick.

'Did they interview you too, in Bethel?' Tikaani asked.

'Yeah, I talked to a couple of reporters briefly,' Beck replied. 'But you are the real story, buddy.' He had seen his friend on almost every news bulletin.

'When does your own film crew get here?' Tikaani asked Uncle Al.

'Later this afternoon,' he replied. 'We're finally going to make our documentary – but I'm not sure it's needed now.'

For a moment Tikaani looked thunderstruck. 'Not needed? Why not?' He had actually gone pale.

'It looks like Anakat already has someone to speak for it.'

Tikaani frowned. 'Who? I . . .' His eyes went wide and he flushed. 'Oh! Me?'

Beck smiled. He'd already had Al point this out to him, at length, on the helicopter ride here.

It had been unfortunate – for the reporters – that Beck and Tikaani hadn't stayed together. But it hadn't stopped the news coverage, though. HERO TEENS BATTLE BLIZZARD TO SAVE UNCLE! That had been just one of the headlines.

But – maybe because Tikaani had been on his own when the news crews descended on Anakat – something interesting had happened. Tikaani became the one they concentrated on. Every time he talked on TV he said a little more about preserving Anakat. And now the news companies seemed more interested in that than in their journey across the mountains.

'You're a young American and a young Anak,' Al explained to him. 'You've got a foot in both camps. You understand them both and you help them both understand each other. I've seen it happening in the last week. You've managed to become the Anak youth spokesman for the environment.'

Tikaani flushed deeper. 'I . . . I really don't want to be. I just want to . . . you know' – he waved hand around generally – 'save Anakat.'

'Good on you. You've got to use that media interest,' Al said cheerfully. 'And while it is there, you're going to do a lot of good. You already have.'

'Enough to stop Lumos?' Beck asked.

And Al shrugged. 'Who knows, Beck? Who knows?'

* * *

When they got back to Tikaani's house, his dad was there with the satellite phone in his hand. 'Call for you, Professor,' he said. 'It's your producer.'

'James?' Al frowned. 'What does he want? He's meant to be on the helicopter right now.' He took the phone. 'James? What gives?'

A pause.

'*What?* Says who? . . . Right . . .'

His eyes flitted over the boys and he turned away, as if he wanted privacy and somehow it made a difference when they were standing two metres away from him.

'Can you confirm . . . ? Right. Yes. Excellent. I'll see to it. Bye.'

He hung up and stood there for a moment, his face clouded and deep in thought. Then he pulled a notepad out of his pocket, sat down and began to write.

'Do me a favour, boys,' he said. He tore the sheet out of the pad, folded it, and gave it to Beck. 'You can run faster than me. Give this to that lovely young lady Tikaani was just talking to. It may be in all our interests.'

Beck took the paper, bursting to know what was in it. Al pierced him with a look.

'Go!'

And the boys ran off with the message.

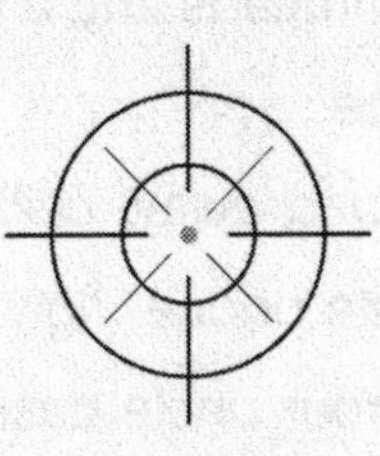

CHAPTER 46

The film crew was packing up where they had left them. Joanne had been filming herself asking the same questions she had just asked Tikaani, so that when the interview was broadcast they could mix the questions and answers together.

'Hi, guys.' She greeted them with a smile. They had broken the Inuit rule and run. 'Where's the fire?'

They smiled and Beck handed her the paper.

'From my uncle,' he said.

She looked sidelong at him. 'Alan Granger? Well, well. Maybe he's asking me on a date.' She unfolded the paper casually, swept it with a glance, and went rigid. Then she read it again more carefully. 'Do . . . you guys know what this is?'

They shook their heads and a mischievous smile spread over her face.

'Right.' She turned away, calling for one of her crew. 'Dave! Satellite phone, right now . . . And you guys? Wait there. Your uncle basically wants me to run a question through some of my contacts and I may have an answer for him . . .'

Whatever she had to say over the phone, she said it so they couldn't hear, though there was much glancing over to where they were waiting. Beck was beginning to feel just a *little* irritated . . .

But after five minutes she seemed to get the answer she wanted. 'And that's definite?' she asked the phone. 'One hundred per cent, bona fide, guaranteed? . . . I owe you. I owe you big time . . . Right. Get me a two-minute slot on tonight's show . . . ' Kay – bye.' She hung up and turned to the crew. 'Camera! Mike!' she called. 'Over here, right now! Now, guys, if you could just stand over there, where Tikaani was before . . .'

'You're going to interview us?' Tikaani asked without enthusiasm.

'You bet! You'll see . . .'

And so, a bit confused, they stood side by side with Joanne, their backs to the inlet and facing the camera. The cameraman gave his cue and Joanne spoke into her microphone.

'I'm here in Anakat right now with Tikaani and Beck, whose adventures we've heard all about over the past few days. I'm about to tell them the news you just heard.'

She turned to the boys with a delighted smile.

'So what is your reaction to the breaking news that Lumos Petroleum has abandoned its plans to build a plant here in Anakat?'

Later, they met up in Tikaani's house with the crew who had come to film Al's documentary. The producer had brought a copy of the leaked press release which was the source of the rumour that Lumos Petroleum had changed its plans for Anakat. They sat at the table in the main room and Beck read through it.

'"A spokesman confirmed that the corporation had previously drawn up a number of contingencies, one of which involved building the contested refinery and relocating the Anak people, the inhabitants of the disputed area. 'We see no need for this course of action now,' he said. 'Geological surveys suggest that the surrounding area of Anakat may not be entirely suitable'—"' Beck broke off. Joy and anger struggled together inside him. Joy that thanks to Tikaani – and the groundwork laid by Uncle Al and everyone else – the campaign had borne fruit. Anger that there always had to be an excuse.

'That's not true! They *totally* intended to start drilling here!' Beck exclaimed.

'Of course they did.' Al gently pried the paper out of his hands and quickly scanned it. Beck could almost see the warm glow of pleasure that enveloped him. 'But what were they going to say? "The corporation admitted that everyone was making such a big deal about the two teen heroes that it would be really bad publicity to go ahead"? They pay their PR people a lot to save face.'

'Maybe,' Beck agreed. But it left a bad taste. They *had* meant to build a refinery. They *had* lost the battle. Why couldn't they admit it?

'Beck, we won,' Al said quietly. 'Rather, we won

this one. There'll be plenty more battles. And who knows, maybe they'll make a movie about you two. For the moment it is, as I believe your generation likes to say, sorted.'

'Yes,' Beck said sardonically. He wished Al wouldn't try and use modern slang – it just didn't work. 'It is, like, well sorted, innit?'

Al closed his eyes and sat back in his chair. 'I need to rest for a while, boys. Go have fun . . .'

They strolled down Anakat's main street towards the hall where Tikaani had spoken to the whole village and where a party was now taking place.

'We did it,' he stated simply.

'Yup,' Beck agreed.

And that was all they needed to say. There was enough celebration going on.

'A movie, eh?' Tikaani said reflectively as they walked.

Beck grunted. 'Hmm. They'd have to put a girl in too, of course. There'd need to be a romance element.'

'Really?' Tikaani looked thoughtful, one

eyebrow raised. 'Obviously, I'd be the one who gets her.'

Beck looked sideways at him. 'In. Your. Dreams.'

Tikaani grinned.

They continued to walk companionably towards the party. Word about Lumos Petroleum had definitely spread. Laughter and music was drifting towards them from the hall.

Then something moved in the corner of Beck's vision, just beyond the trees at the edge of the village. A shadow that loped across the ground.

Tikaani put a hand on Beck's arm, staring into the woods. 'Hey, did you see . . . ?'

Beck looked at where the shadow had been, then smiled and turned away. 'The wolves are still watching you, Tikaani.'

'Yeah.' Tikaani looked thoughtfully into the trees. 'I wonder what they have in mind?' He paused for a moment longer, then turned back to the road. 'Well, I'm in the right place for them to find me. I'm home.'

BEAR'S SURVIVAL TIPS

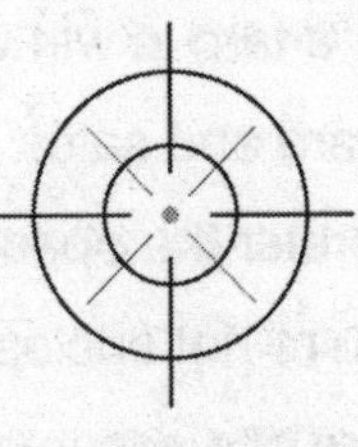

TARPS

In chapter 25 of Way of the Wolf, Beck uses a tarp to create a deck for his make-shift raft. A tarp – or tarpaulin – is a sheet of waterproof material that can be used to create a quick and effective shelter, either for spending the night, or simply for protecting yourself from the elements. It has a number of advantages over a more traditional tent.

- It's lighter, so will keep the weight of your pack down.
- If you try to erect a tent in the rain, you're more than likely to get the inside wet. A tarp shelter can be erected much more quickly and, as there is no floor to get

wet, rain isn't really a problem. It's quick to dry, too.

- Cooking under a tarp in wet weather is straightforward and safe.
- Many people prefer the openness of a tarp shelter – you're not enclosed in canvas so have more of a sense of being in the outdoors.

Tarps can be erected in a number of ways. Common configurations include an A-type roof (elevated or at ground level), a lean-to, over a camp cot or hammock, or any combination of these.

I have used tarps in some very obscure, difficult places, from jungles to swamps, and they have been very useful when needing cover in a hurry. They also provide good space to work in while keeping out of the rain. They don't keep the mozzies out, but a well-placed fire can do that job for you.

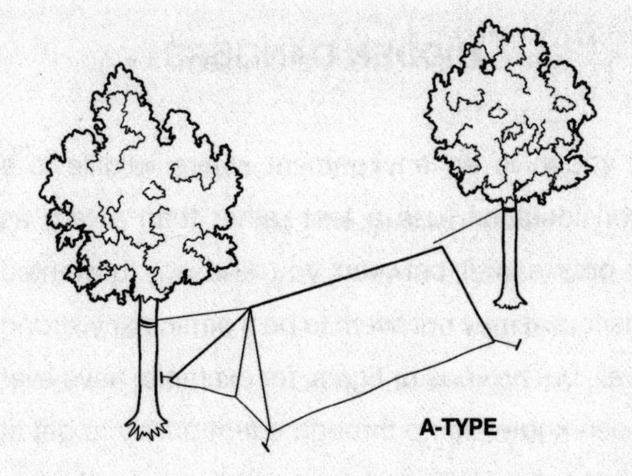
A-TYPE

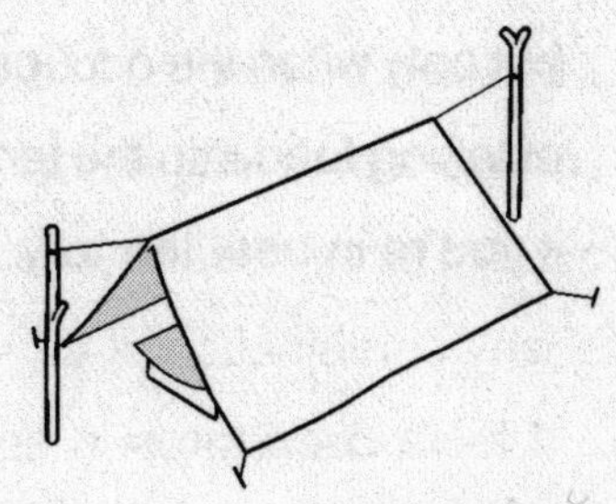
OVER CAMP COT

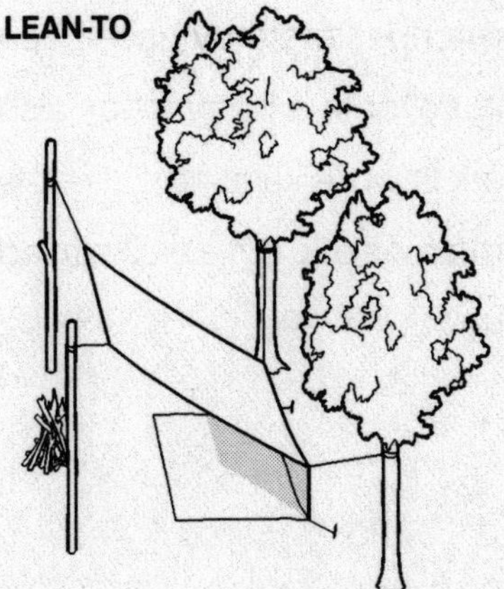
LEAN-TO

HIDDEN DANGERS

If you're in an environment where wildlife is a consideration, use a tent rather than a tarp as it puts a wall between you and any unwanted visitors. It may not seem to be a particularly strong wall, but no lions or tigers, for example, have ever been known to rip through a tent purely to get at the occupant. Bears have been known to do this, but only when the occupant has made the mistake of taking food into the tent with them – a big no-no if you're in bear territory.

Beck Granger will return in . . .

Book 3:

MISSION SURVIVAL

SANDS OF THE SCORPION

Read on for a sneak preview . . .

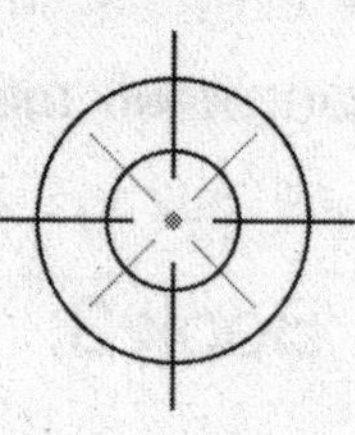

CHAPTER 1

The wheels of the plane thumped down on the runway tarmac. Beck Granger lurched forward in his seat as the brakes bit. The plane shook and its engines roared in reverse. Then abruptly the sound died down and he could sit back again while it turned and trundled onto the taxiway.

Beck breathed out quietly. After his recent adventures in Alaska, air travel still made him more nervous than it should.

Across the aisle his Uncle Al smiled and raised an eyebrow. He knew exactly what was going through Beck's mind. The same crash that had made Beck so nervous had almost killed *him* as well. Beck met his eyes and raised an eyebrow in return.

His friend Peter Grey sat in the window seat on his left. They had pulled the blind down over the window to block out the bright sun during the flight.

'Hey, let's see!'

Peter had flipped up the blind before Beck could stop him. The harsh light of Sierra Leone flooded into the cabin.

'Aargh!'

Peter pulled the blind back down quickly, then flashed a bashful grin at Beck. His eyes were wide behind his round glasses. 'Well, we're here!'

'Yup,' Beck agreed.

'Hold on . . .'

Peter opened his bag and rummaged around in it. Beck rolled his eyes as his friend emerged with his pride and joy, the top-of-the-range digital camera he had got for his birthday. It took photos and filmed video equally well. Peter cautiously pushed the blind up again, not so far this time, and pressed the camera against the window.

'*Look, Mummy*,' Beck said in a high, breathless voice, '*I took a photo of yet another airport terminal and it looked exactly like every other airport terminal I've ever been to!'*

'You're just jealous,' Peter said loftily. He slid the camera into a pouch that was clipped to his belt.

Beck smiled.

They had always bickered. Peter was Beck's oldest friend from school; he was small and slim and looked as though, if the wind blew hard, it might knock him over.

That was probably why older boys had tried to pick on him during their first days at school together. A group of teenage bullies twice Peter's size had tried to make him hand over the money in his pocket. They had expected him to be a pushover. What they hadn't expected was that Peter would just say no. He didn't cower. He didn't run away. He didn't fight back. He just refused, and kept on refusing. He simply would not be frightened by the group crowding round him.

Beck had watched in fascination, ready to intervene on Peter's side if it got violent. It became even more fascinating when he worked out what was going on. After five minutes of attempted intimidation he had realized that Peter was playing with them. He had got them to a point where they were telling him what they needed the money for. They had stopped trying to frighten him. Now he was just showing them up as the morons they were, and they were too dim to understand it.

More and more boys had gathered round to watch. Finally the bullies realized, in the dim recesses of their tiny minds, that half the junior school were laughing at them. They left Peter alone after that.

Peter didn't look much, but Beck recognized that he was brave and determined – and sometimes simply stubborn.

The plane had now come to a standstill and the cabin doors were opened. Warm, humid air flooded in to do battle with the plane's air conditioning. The forty-odd passengers clambered to their feet, picked up their bags and shuffled out into the equatorial sunshine.

* * *

The three of them – Beck, Peter and Al, or Professor Sir Alan Granger as he was better known – had flown from London to Freetown, Sierra Leone's capital.

Then they had boarded this smaller plane to fly up country, near to the border with Guinea.

Al was attending a conference on African tribal peoples. They used traditional methods of sustenance that had kept their societies going for thousands of years. The western world had all but forgotten how to farm sustainably. The purpose of the conference was to see what could be learned from these ancient methods.

Al had taken Beck, of course, because he took Beck everywhere. After Beck's parents had disappeared in that fatal plane crash when he was so young, Al had taken the boy in and raised him like a son.

As for Peter, his parents had recently had another baby. He referred to his new little sister as 'The Bundle'. Beck knew he kept a photo of the baby in his wallet, so he was probably much fonder of her than he let on.

'The Bundle' had been born prematurely and was still quite weak, so the Greys hadn't been able to take their usual summer holiday this year. Peter's parents were advised not to do any travelling with her for the time being. So Beck had invited Peter along on this trip too – he would enjoy the company while Al was ensconced in the conference centre and talking to tribal leaders.

After that, the three of them planned to travel up to Morocco for a real holiday.

* * *

It wasn't a big modern airport. There was no tunnel from the plane to take them straight into the terminal. They had to walk down some steps and head out across the tarmac, squinting in the sunlight.

It was the first time they had spent any time outdoors since leaving London. Beck took a deep breath of African air. A hot, dry wind blew on his face. It came from the northeast. He worked out the direction by pointing the hour hand of his watch at the sun: halfway between that and twelve o'clock would be south. They were still in the northern hemisphere, he remembered; the direction-finding technique would be accurate. Beck realized that the wind came from the Sahara, only a few hundred miles away.

The Sahara covered a quarter of the African continent. It was vast – almost as big as all of the

USA. The air Beck was breathing had blown across some of the driest land on the planet. It was cooling down now that it had reached the savannah of Sierra Leone's border country, but it still carried a harsh message. It warned that there was a large part of the continent where only the very foolish or the very brave would venture. Or, Beck thought, the very wise – the ones who really knew how to survive there. People like the Berbers, the Tuareg, the Bedouin, who lived and breathed the desert life as naturally as Beck would cross the road back home.

Well, the closest Beck planned to come to the Sahara was when they flew over it en route to Morocco.

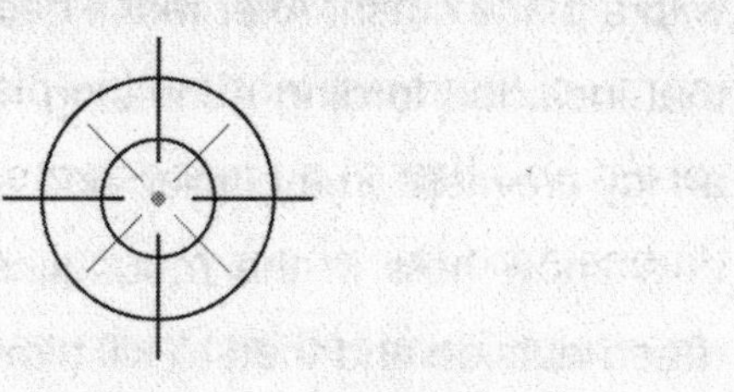

CHAPTER TWO

Peter stumbled into Beck. 'Oops! Sorry!'

He had his camera out again and was panning it around the airport. He had been walking backwards and hadn't seen Beck standing there.

'Just taking some pics of the plane,' he added, by way of explanation.

Beck grinned and looked back. 'Yeah, well, it got us here. That's all I really ask a plane to do.'

Peter suddenly flushed red. 'Hey, I'm sorry. I wasn't thinking.'

Beck frowned. 'Huh?'

'I mean, you and' – Peter gestured – 'planes. You know . . .'

Beck smiled knowingly. Peter was referring to his recent Alaskan adventure, which had started with a plane crash. After that it had turned into a trek that included fording a freezing river, crawling over an icy crevasse in a glacier, and spending the night in a snow hole in the mountains while a blizzard raged outside and tried to kill him.

The enquiry into the crash had put it down to failure of the plane's single engine.

'I'm fine with planes,' he insisted – but couldn't resist adding, 'as long as they've got more than one engine. I count 'em carefully before I get on nowadays.'

Peter wasn't quite sure how he was meant to react to that, but when he saw Beck grinning, he relaxed into a laugh.

They collected their bags and emerged into the chaos of the town.

A battered old shuttle bus carried them to their hotel. Beck reckoned it was at least as old as he was: splits in the seats were covered up with rough tape and it lurched from side to side as the driver navigated the traffic, one hand permanently clamped down on the horn. Judging by the din, every other driver seemed to take the same approach.

The roads were packed – mostly with equally battered trucks and lorries, and the occasional gleaming new Jeep or Land Cruiser. This was a culture where, if you had wealth, it was obvious. And there were taxis, hundreds of them, threading their way between the other cars with suicidal ease. Every driver seemed to regard other road users as potential enemies.

There was no air con. The windows were wide open and the spicy, dry air blew through the cabin. It couldn't quite get rid of the smell of stuffy, hot vehicle.

Beck loved it. What was the point of being abroad, he often thought, if you tried to make it exactly like home? The only way to enjoy a town in Africa was to treat it like a town in Africa. Just soak it all in.

He glanced over at Peter and wondered what he made of it. His friend had never been outside Europe before. He chuckled to himself. Peter, of course, was leaning out of the window with his camera pressed to his eye. He seemed to be loving it.

* * *

'Hey! A fan!'

It was the first thing Peter said when they stepped into their hotel room. A large three-bladed ceiling fan hummed lazily in the warm air. The room had twin beds and a bathroom off to one side. Gauze curtains billowed gently in the open windows. They filtered the harsh sunlight and helped keep out the insects.

'And a minibar!' Peter checked the cabinet and his face only fell a little. 'Locked.' He ran over to the windows and found a door out to the balcony. He fought his way past the curtains. 'Cool – and a *swimming pool*!'

Beck still hadn't got further than the door. 'And a friend left with both suitcases . . .' he muttered quietly.

He lugged the cases into the room and dropped his own on the bed nearest the window. If Peter wasn't going to make his own choice, he decided, then *he* would.

There was a simple room-service menu on the table between the two beds. Beck picked it up and scanned it quickly. 'No, sorry,' he called. 'This just won't do. We're moving.'

Peter was back inside in a flash. 'We've got to move?' he asked in surprise.

Beck brandished the menu. 'You know there's not a single insect on this? It won't be a holiday without some sort of survival food,' he said with a deadpan expression.

It took Peter a moment to work out he was being wound up. He loved hearing about everything Beck had had to eat on his Alaskan adventure. 'Oh, ha ha! But, c'mon. Look at the pool!'

Beck let his friend pull him out onto the balcony to look at a grassy lawn ringed with weary-looking palm trees and a swimming pool nestled in the middle. It sparkled with clear blue water. The din of the town was blocked out by the bulk of the building. The garden was peaceful, and the pool looked cool and inviting.

'OK,' he agreed. 'Last one in's a sissy . . .'

* * *

'Beck, Peter,' said Al, raising his voice slightly over the restaurant's background chatter, 'this is our hostess, Mrs Chalobah.'

The open-air restaurant was in an adjacent

courtyard. The air was pleasantly cool at this time of day. Candles burned on the tables to ward off insects, and the smells of spicy food drifted on the breeze. The bow-tied waiter had led them through the tables to where Mrs Chalobah, the conference organizer, was already seated. Although Beck had heard plenty about this lady, he had never met her. Now she rose to greet them. She wore brightly coloured robes and headdress and a huge beam on her face.

'Alan! So good to see you!'

Mrs Chalobah kissed Al on both cheeks, and then turned her wide African smile onto the two boys. They shifted slightly uncomfortably: Al had made them dress up in jackets and ties. Beck hoped that it was the only time he would have to wear them on the entire holiday.

'My, two such handsome young men! Here, sit down. Tell me all about your journey . . .'

If she had asked Beck, he would have said something simple like 'Fine, thank you. We got on an aeroplane and we flew to Freetown.' He had met adults who were able to chat endlessly about nothing but he had never mastered the art.

But she had been looking at Peter. Peter could describe the flight from Heathrow as if it was the first flight ever from London to Sierra Leone. He talked, and she encouraged him along with smiles and nods. Beck and Al exchanged looks. Al winked. Beck was warming to Mrs Chalobah.

Then he heard Peter's innocent question:

'Is Mr Chalobah coming tonight?'

Beck saw his uncle wince and guessed it was not the question to ask. Mrs Chalobah's cheerful expression faltered a little.

'Mr Chalobah will not be joining us.' She said it with a simple, sad dignity. Even Peter noticed that there was more to be said – she was just finding the right words. He kept quiet and let her continue at her own pace.

'One of the many problems our country faces is that there are people who would take its wealth to use for their own ends. My husband believed that the money from our diamond industry should be used to bring benefit to Sierra Leone. We are a developing country and that development must be paid for somehow! But' – she sighed – 'there are those – ruthless, wicked people – who take what does not belong to them, make themselves rich, leaving the rest of us to struggle in the dirt.'

'Do you mean smugglers?' Beck asked.

She glanced at him, and nodded with a grave bow of her head. 'I mean smugglers,' she confirmed. 'They are the scourge of this country.'

'Mr Chalobah was a judge . . .' Al began.

'He was a judge,' she said, still with that quiet dignity, 'who sentenced one of the worst of these smugglers to thirty years in jail and confiscated his stolen wealth. His associates took revenge. A thousand mourners came to my husband's funeral, from all walks of life. Friends, complete strangers, even some criminals he had previously sentenced for other crimes – but all united in their contempt for his murderers and their respect for a good man.'

She looked each of them earnestly in the eye. 'Peter, Beck . . . these people I speak of are not nice people at all. They shame the people of Africa. And they are well organized. Their web of evil spreads over the entire continent, and beyond. But with the help of people like your uncle' – she squeezed Al's hand, and suddenly her good mood was back – 'who is a very nice person, and with the help of this conference, hopefully we can make progress and leave these dark times behind us once and for all.'

They all raised their glasses – wine for Mrs Chalobah and Al, fresh fruit juice for the boys – and together they drank a toast to the future.

BEAR GRYLLS is one of the world's most famous adventurers. After spending three years in the SAS he set off to explore the globe in search of even bigger challenges. He has climbed Mount Everest, crossed the Sahara Desert and circumnavigated Britain on a jet-ski. His TV shows have been seen by more than 1.2 billion viewers in more than 150 countries. In 2009, Bear became Chief Scout to the Scouting Association. He lives in London and Wales with his wife Shara and their three sons: Jesse, Marmaduke and Huckleberry.